S0-BZV-283

2.45

THE COAT

...STORES OF AMERICA, IN...
4714 Main Street
Lisle, IL 60532

Other books by Hugo Charteris

A SHARE OF THE WORLD
MARCHING WITH APRIL
PICNIC AT POROKORRO
THE LIFELINE
PICTURES ON THE WALL
THE RIVERWATCHER
THE INDIAN SUMMER OF GABRIEL MURRAY

For children

CLUNIE
STAYING WITH AUNT ROZZIE

THE COAT

Hugo Charteris

HARCOURT, BRACE & WORLD, INC.
New York

Copyright © 1966 by Hugo Charteris

All rights reserved.
No part of this publication may be reproduced
or transmitted in any form or by any means,
electronic or mechanical, including photocopy, recording,
or any information storage and retrieval system,
without permission in writing from the publisher.

First American edition 1970

Library of Congress Catalog Card Number: 74-100499

Printed in the United States of America

I

A sudden crash gave rise to a whistling, diminishing roar. Pigeons scattered from messy ledges and careered over flying-buttress, cobbles, top-hats and statue. Boys looked up, interested by a Spitfire clearing the school-clock by a yard. Such familiarity suggested an old boy—already doing 360 m.p.h. War was a short cut.

A quaint figure in mortar-board and gown, half-way up chapel steps, fought like an auctioneer against the distraction: 'Landers, Lapperton, Law, Lowinski . . .'

At every name a top-hat was raised in proof of the owner's presence. 'Mr. Loxley . . .'

The plane appeared between spires, climbing and turning.

'. . . MISTER LOXLEY,' repeated the master as though about to bring down the hammer.

Before it was too late the tail-coated crowd was jostled open and there stood an untidy youth holding aloft a top-hat that was creased with maltreatment. 'Here, sir,' he shouted and then turned, smiling in response to surrounding smiles, as much as to say: what's the flap, I did it again, and put his hat on at a brave angle, an angle that suited his black curls.

Then there was elbowing and hissing: 'He's talking to you.'

Tim Loxley turned again, affecting the indifference of the hard case. But his big eyes looked scared.

'Mister Loxley!' The figure on the steps uttered the prefix 'Mr.' (meaning in this place 'Honourable') uncomfortably which rubbed in what everyone knew, that only war explained his presence. 'You're to report to the school office, at once.'

The boys muttered.

Such a big departure from custom was rare; even in war. Only ten yards away the Founder protruded unmoved from a mound of sandbags, sceptre in one hand, orb in the other. Business was as usual, ' Absence ' as usual. The fact that they were all carrying gas-masks in cartons like a lot of undertakers with duty-free, airport whisky made no difference. Old Asquith up there on the steps must be out of his mind.

Someone mimicked him sotto voce. The man was tantalising bait: something about him of the failed actor suddenly forced to play Hamlet at seventy; groping for a solemnity, which he grudged to Eton and ridiculed in himself, but which perforce he offered to his employers and charges simply because he had to offer something.

Yes, surely a mistake!

The boys now looked hopeful: what further gaffe might he not commit; with luck the whole Absence might dissolve in a congenial riot. Didn't he know that he should have said 'Wait behind'?

Perhaps it was something to do with Loxley's father . . .

'Ask him why,' someone hissed at Loxley—but it was too late, the old voice was off again, descending the rungs of that long ladder of names, English, foreign, titled, names that he mispronounced, often leaning absurdly in the direction of pedantry, so he got many a mutter of laughter . . . 'Lumsden, Lutch-yens, Lyttelton.'

Loxley moved off kicking a cobble, hands in pockets, smiling, living up to a reputation. The school office was almost his address. He had to go there every morning to sign a book ten minutes before early school: and only a year ago he had hung about outside it with two members of Sixth Form who were to hold up his shirt-tails when the Lower Master birched him. In the event the older boys had performed their task with fortitude and afterwards the tall, wild-eyed octogenarian, muttering gratefully, had kissed him, adding insult to injury. The smart and shame still stung though he knew it helped that idea of himself which existed in the minds of his fellows. Others of his age already had caps, long coloured scarves trailing to the ground, asterisks after their name in the school list denoting prizes, distinctions and what not—he had a notoriety, which like caps, could elicit envy. Even when he was handed back an exercise rent down the middle and livid with red ink, faces turned back towards him half-marvelling at his smile, that shy, rather dopey, disdainful smile, which he exploited.

Tail-coated bodies moved aside for him like those that once made an aisle to Tyburn: what had Loxley done now? Tim Loxley, son of the Minister of Fuel!

For a nearby friend the sensational possibilities were too much. 'Tim—wait and I'll be with you.'

This boy, like Tim, belonged to a group who all knew each other in the holidays and whose parents were very rich. Another highest common factor, apart from money, was transatlantic: they all knew Churchills, Astors, and Douglas Fairbanks.

Here, whatever their discrepancies in age, they consorted mainly with each other, thus creating a vertical group cutting across the horizontal grain of school custom and even of natural law. Their bond was basic. Rationing had so far not touched them. At week-ends huge cars still took them so far and fast out of bounds that they were never caught. Even Eton, accustomed to digesting princes, could not absorb this juvenile money-club.

Indeed by involving them in a world apart where barbaric strength and even brains could put a pauper on top, the place had forced them back upon themselves, forced them to talk a language that deferred to the holidays when anything under the sun, not least the sun itself and even a rather spurious prestige, was still available.

'Tim——!'

Another half-broken alto offered support in return for revelation. But Tim was not so facile. The drama of his perpetual delinquency along with dinosaurs were his two cards, even with his own kind. They needed secrecy to seem a royal flush. His slow, ambiguous smile raised the stakes to incredible possibilities: rape of the Latvian refugee kitchen-maid, the knickers perhaps of his housemaster's daughter flying from School Hall instead of the Royal Standard. He passed through them all, yielding nothing.

In fact a cold snake of fear had coiled in his guts: a memory of another school-day at a different school four . . . five years ago, interrupted by an equally abnormal request to report (to matron, it had been that time). She had given him an extra cup of cocoa and then told him his mother was dead.

He kicked a cobble so hard it drew a look from a member of Pop, a tall boy with a carnation in his button-hole who had been smiling to himself as he walked.

Tim sloped into the familiar, fusty darkness. Black tin boxes, padlocks, leather-bound ledgers, the old iron inkstand with a quill pen and the messenger called Grablick, all seemed to be waiting for Charles Dickens and the next damned holiday task.

'Well, Grablick,' said Tim in the tone of a tolerant despot: 'When you've finished plotting in the shadows perhaps you'll tell me why I'm wanted.'

Grablick was large, breathless and apathetic. Gassed at Ypres he bore himself with the air of one who had long ago stopped trying to understand. Perhaps for this reason a rare dignity attached to his person here.

When he moved he wheezed and jingled with keys.

'Here y'are, sir,' he said and handed over a twisted morsel of paper. ' 'Ope it's better than usual.'

The comment was offered in a tone of encouragement: as it were from slave to slave. Too often in the past he had been for Loxley the messenger of punishing authority, supervising his signature, inscribing his name on bills of malefactors and even putting a rod for him, if not in pickle, then at least on the second shelf down where the safe hid it from sight, the thing by now being somewhat shameful. Yes, he told tourists, the Lower Master won't have it lying around where boys pass remarks about the length to the boy that's getting it.

'*What's this*,' Tim protested, 'a fag's message,' and he held the paper before Grablick demanding veteran acknowledgment that here in the School Office was a message *from* a boy *for* a boy.

'So we've come to this, Grablick,' Tim continued in the tone of grave disappointment which was so familiar to him: 'My brother, Viscount Crowle, president of Pop and Captain of the Eleven, gives orders to the Masters—and they're only too pleased to oblige!"

Grablick wheezed and shifted away.

Tim read out, 'Come to my room before six. It's urgent. C.'

'That's it then,' Grablick said, relieved for him. 'You're all right.'

' "C.",' quoted Tim. 'Do you ever sign yourself G., Grablick?'

Grablick raised one hand again a little way for mercy. He wished to be exempted from honesty. It was a luxury.

Tim drifted out into the tide of boys ebbing now in small waves from the high-water marks of Absence. Some called to him, challenging him. But he said nothing, moved on, hat still tilted, tie still dangling, hands in pockets, proceeding like a penny-for-the-guy boy towards his imperious destination.

2

'All of you here'—shouted the bent old Dean in the long aisle—you here—the echoes took him up on high, as though endorsing him on the spot. And he stopped, the pause making it plain he was breaking into peroration; he took another step back towards the altar from which he had slowly limped. 'All of you here are *privileged*. Privileged materially, privileged culturally and privileged spiritually . . .' Rapid-fire of tongue twisters imposed no strain; he separated each like a volley, and for each faced a different point of the compass. The echoes fairly sang and some boys even listened, compelled for the most part as though by Gielgud or Gracie Fields. Encouraged, the voice carried on, harking back to the parable of the good steward to whom so much had been given and from whom so much would be required.

The signs of restlessness which normally marked the last phase of a Sunday sermon died away. Young eyes fixed on the agile, old face with its lizard-like skin. '*We are at war!*' it cried. Names of war-dead were embossed in gun-metal all round. Fathers, uncles galore . . . Now a sudden blue octave lower: 'and so from *you* to whom so much has been given . . . *much* . . .' the Dean pivoted like a gunman in a Western 'MUCH . . .' then his voice perished like a punctured balloon as though he disdained to say clear what they would be damned if they didn't know well already '. . . will be required.'

The last syllable rose a musical third.

Tim in that time had drawn Jurassic Stegasaurus, fascinated as ever by the similarity of its head to its tail.

But not so his brother, Peter . . .

Who now waited for him in his room, pacing calmly, considering his own destiny. It was taking shape, dimly rising to-day from the mists of childhood and adolescence, bearing a remarkable resemblance to the view that others had always held of him: a hero, a boy, as the Dean said, to whom much had been given and from whom much would be required.

So far—a century against Winchester and the Newcastle Scholarship . . . Something already autumnal and melancholy in the fullness of his success; something almost *dead* . . . made him think of himself as a 'good king,' who had less chance than others of 'living.'

The process had started early: appearance, physique and that which the sort of people he knew called 'charm,' then worse still: modesty. (They had to tell him even that! To his face!) Something missing all the time. A century in his first match for his private school, and so on, all honours and without great effort. Then, cooped up, this schoolboy Alexander had sought new worlds, the outer world, for salvation, to women and at Cannes quickly acquired a divorcée mistress who was coveted by sensualists. He overstressed the nature of his magic wand: the industrial empire waiting for him. Lately he had climbed out of his house at night, on one occasion attending early school in a dinner-jacket roughly concealed by scarf and coat. But even when he was seen he could not be caught (the maid had winked and said she hadn't seen anyone). He sought contact: to have been caught would have been contact. When he looked at people they conspired to reflect him, make him look at himself. So every face was a cul-de-sac.

Now at last something different! The noise of the Spitfire

had confirmed the promise of a little fresh air; unlike the voice of his father on the trunk line which still echoed in his head, claiming, even at this eleventh hour and when he had already been accepted by the R.A.F., that the Phantoms were a much more adventurous unit than any fighter squadron.

Some elation came into Peter's grey-blue eyes as he remembered the raving intensity of his father's protest, the hoarse squeal with which that massive man had claimed that the Phantoms were 'already training in Ireland' as though this constituted some obscure panache, alibi perhaps—or sporting attraction. But then his father had given himself away, reeling off the names of about ten oldest sons and heirs, most of them known personally to Peter. 'Don't you want to be with your friends?'

Peter had said, 'I want to fly.'

Then he had let the wild words roar round his ears, holding the receiver away from his head, feeling that already things were a bit better till the incredible climax: '*Don't you realise the Germans may be here by Christmas.*' This had shocked him. Six inches from his nose there was a sticker: *Careless talk costs lives.*

From there: the business about Tim . . .

Something had happened to him as he listened.

Now he paced up and down with the humble, joyful sensation which comes in those rare moments when suddenly a person recognises some part of himself that is second-hand. He felt freer. In fact flying—already.

3

Tim was in no hurry.

Fison's was a smelly house: carbolic and cricket pads, urine and cabbage as the door hissed, sagged, shut. A voice yelled between the cold, naked walls.

Tim passed the notice-board covered with ghastly decrees, official threats and adjustments to war, A.R.P., L.D.V., and a quartet from Munich with four signatures below.

A few boys slouched by the slab, deep in their elbows, leaning right forward over *Daily Mirrors* and Jane; two vied with each in the rough competitive voice of adolescence, keeping violent contradiction friendly and obscenity meaningless, pure. They took in pretty Tim with his big clear eyes and ivory skin and one of them who knew him said, 'Hi! Tim—the great man's in, if that's what you want.'

'Well tell him I wish to see him down here at once, will you.'

They smiled, then, at the difference between these two who were brothers.

Tim went up the stairs past the lettering of old names on blackened wood. In 1865 Charman-Hewitt had been Captain here. Tim congratulated this skeleton. Eton: all as usual, the strange names on strange doors, then a familiar name, different Fire Orders, linoleum newer, somewhere the sound of wrestling so that he thought: it's true: my brother doesn't give a hoot; doesn't beat much, doesn't fag much.

'Well C.,' he said as he breezed in on the Holy of Holies.

As usual you could hardly breathe with the amount of wool there was hanging about, ten-foot coloured scarves festooned from every hook, caps on the corners of Peter Scott pictures, duck, geese and sunsets and ribboned lists on every square inch of wall, one criss-crossed with canes as though the rules had been forged on furrowed buttocks with splintered bamboo; then the Rogues Gallery—just 42,000 pictures of Charles, John, Adrian, Mitch, Jules, Hassan, Bud, Christopher, with a straight fifty per cent in Pop clothes and some poor twirps who had presumed to submit to Peter their image without even a stick-up tie, and others who had sought safety in mufti.

'What's the flap?' and he sat down on the ottoman, hat still on and feet stretched far out: you had to protect yourself.

'You're going to America to-morrow,' Peter said and stationed himself before the fire, facing his younger brother and looking at him strangely.

'Come again.'

Peter obliged.

Tim said, 'Are we more than usually nuts? I mean heck,' like Bob Hope and scratched his head pushing his top-hat so far forward that it obscured his eyes. Then he took it off, and laid it beside him. 'Look, Crowle. I suggest you start at the beginning.'

Peter said, 'Evacuees: slum children go to Garston, you go to America.'

Garston was their home.

'And where are *you* going?'

'You know.'

'I thought Pa said you couldn't . . .'

Peter smiled faintly.

Tim was impressed. 'You mean you *did* tell him to put his head in a bucket.'

Such a feat, in the case of their mutual parent, transcended imagination. But that was the way with Peter's feats . . . he hit Gubby Allen's fastest ball straight along the ground a foot from Allen's ankle so hard the man never bothered to reach for it but merely walked across to mid-off and took a rest while all the pretty girls cooed and got their legs up two hundred yards away. Now he told Pa to stuff it. Tim supposed, it made sense of a rather morbid kind. But Our Crowle, needless to say, showed no triumph: That would have been boasting.

He just said, 'I go in December.'

Tim stole a look then at his elder brother: but the dazzle was too much. All that fancy dress! The chrysanthemum button-hole, the violet silk waistcoat, the gold watch chain.

'So I shall be the Earl of Bewick,' Tim said.

'I suppose that's the object of the operation,' Peter said, and he looked out of the window at the yellowing chestnuts and the rose-coloured wall covered with fallen leaves.

'*I'm sending Tim to New York to-morrow* . . .' his father had yelled as though this were his last card and the Ace of Trumps!

'What's funny?' Tim said.

Peter began pacing again. 'You're to be ready at twelve to-morrow. Charlie's picking you up. You go to London where you collect your stuff. Then Poppy takes you to Liverpool where you join a convoy.'

'Poppy . . .' Tim said dully.

With the mention of that name, he was able for the first time to believe a little in what his brother proposed.

'Yes, Poppy.' Peter looked at him.

'So Poppy's coming?' Tim said avoiding his brother's eyes. He picked up a cricket bat and holding it between his legs bumped the end up and down gently on the carpet.

'No. She's not.'

The bat stayed put, on the floor. Peter went on, 'You're

meeting someone who's taking over another child . . . A Cubitt.'

'Have a *heart*!'

Peter's voice changed and he said, 'How d'you feel about it?'

Tim got a sense of occasion. Never before had Peter asked his opinion. But he couldn't oblige.

'What do *you* think of it?' he said helplessly.

Peter was silent for a long time. At last he said:

'I'm glad I'm not you!'

Tim's heart sank, though his brother smiled.

'Thanks,' he said coldly. 'But possibly I shall be eating fudge when you're pushing up the daisies in some corner of a foreign field.'

Peter's smile faded. Not two feet from where he stood, covered by a blotter was a poem in his own hand, echoing Brooke and Julian Grenfell.

And Tim suddenly thought, 'I probably *shall* be Lord Crowle.'

The idea was agreeable though it would mean Peter dead. He looked at the braided edge of his brother's black tail-coat.

Then Tim thought, No, he'll mow them down. Richthofen. The lot. He'll come over to the States and get a ticker-tape welcome with gongs from shoulder to shoulder, and a girl on each arm, as in the picture of him at home, when the Ballet came to Manchester. He and this Douglas Bader chap, in the *Illustrated London News*.

'Who else is going with you?' Tim said.

Peter mentioned one name unknown to Tim, a boy not in any of the teams or anything. But that was C. all over.

Silence fell, uneasy, heavy with the incredible future which seemed suddenly to have leapt on them both out of life as usual.

Tim tried again to see it: Liverpool with Poppy, New York

with 'a Cubitt' . . . He felt strangely dispossessed. No proper tea to-morrow . . .

The end of the bat thumped gently on the carpet again as he stared.

Something like this had happened once before . . . He frowned.

'You'll be all right,' Peter said suddenly.

'Where am I going to live?' Tim said with a touch of aggression. 'The White House?'

Peter was dismissive: 'Bluey Bain. . . . You'll probably have a marvellous time. Plenty of flicks . . .' and he smiled.

It was not meant as a taunt. Which made it worse.

'Thanks,' Tim said. 'I'll enjoy them.'

When Tim was sick of his fossils in the holidays, he got Charlie, the chauffeur, to take him to the flicks.

Charlie was his closest companion.

'Do I get home for the holidays?'

Peter moved away from his brother restlessly.

'The North Sea Fleet will be sent to fetch you.'

Peter's tone was tight with sudden impatience, almost grudge. His heart had hardened against his father. Now, less than ever, did the idea of dying depress him. On the contrary he derived satisfaction from it as though it alone would prevent the colossal cheque with which life had presented him at birth from bouncing. Pericles, Rupert Brooke! To him they were of the same family. Perhaps his father had educated him unsuitably.

'Is that all?' Tim said listlessly.

And that was all.

They shook hands sheepishly and gave up in the middle, laughing.

'It was nice knowing you,' Tim said.

That night Tim slammed his door and, wishing to speak to

no one of his impending departure, shut himself up with *Early Mammals*, sunk right back into his basket chair which creaked every now and again when he added a briquette to his fire. No one else, the Dame had told him, had seen fit to supplement their coal ration with briquettes. 'More fool them, ma'am,' he had drawled and with his own hands twice a week carried half a sack of them from a lorry to a hide behind the rubbish bins which the odd-man for a consideration had agreed to overlook. 'Flapper-paps', as Miss Marlow was called, nosed around but never got past the idea that he imported briquettes daily from Windsor. To-night he used them for the last time, piling on as many as possible, unwilling that anyone should inherit them.

The word 'happiness' had not yet entered Tim's large vocabulary. Indeed he was irritated when people asked him if he was happy at Eton. He didn't really know what they were talking about and resented the assumption that they made sense. Something was missing, yes, but something always had been missing and presumably always would be. The real danger was boredom. His tone proclaimed it, a glint in his far-away stare aspired to a kink or two, unspecified; his restless and ready contempt announced shortcoming in every bleak valuation of the things he had to do, cricket, football, maths, Latin Unseen. Now this—evacuation to America. . . .

He frowned sometimes as though the present moment still had the face to tug his concentration from the sluggish colossi of eighty million years ago.

4

A Home Office car driven by a Fanny drew up before the Dorchester. Lord Bewick pulled himself out and grunted as he passed through saluting commissionaires. Doors were opened for him long before he reached them and even before he was in sight of the lift it had been summoned and somehow managed to open its doors in time for him to pass through, along with a page carrying his key. Other people were approaching at the same moment but the lift-boy had no time for them, sealing off Lord Bewick and his key-bearer with a small protective arm and whisking him up out of sight.

On his landing he walked behind the key-bearer with a troubled face. Already he knew from the presence of the page with the key that Poppy hadn't arrived. Nevertheless he peered into her room—seeing what he expected, complete impersonal, untouched unlived-in tidyness. Then he lowered his great bulk beside her cream-coloured telephone and barked at the operator to get him Garston 204—and a moment later he was hectoring his butler for the time and manner of his wife's departure. He wanted to hear that she had left by the evening train. Instead it was by car—after breakfast. He rang off without a word of valediction, and then sat like a figure in some modern version of Dante's *Inferno*, surrounded by the stale-smelling unaired fug of the powerful central heating and a few duplicate items of Poppy's face programme.

Now he knew it: he had gone too far with Peter. It had brought him bad luck; brought him this: no Poppy!

Conducted as the conversation had been from his room in Whitehall to the telephone kiosk in Pop-room at Eton, there had been no inhibiting influence in the shape of listeners. Now he wished there had been . . . Peter's mother, someone at any rate to caution him against driving the boy *out of reach*.

He began having another, happier, more reasonable conversation with his son—a conversation that ended with Peter doing what he had always done, fitting in: excelling and surviving. *As arranged!* It was October . . . Only a year ago, in a private room at Rowlands, he had proposed Peter's health at the champagne breakfast which he, Bertrand, had thrown to celebrate his son's election to Pop. 'My good boy!' he had said. Poppy had told him to keep away; Poppy had said he was probably the first father ever to give such a breakfast. Why shouldn't he? All round the table had been faces he knew, boys he had had to stay at Garston and put in the best stands at the shoots with just such a moment in mind. Why shouldn't he be there when his ship came in?

Now this! He wanted to cry. Cry *to* someone. But to whom? The Home Secretary was a Socialist, the Duke of Suffolk was in America.

And Poppy. Where was Poppy?

He began crying—slowly, sitting quite still on the edge of the empty bed.

Son of the seventeenth Earl of Bewick and a Spanish opera singer, his sense of superiority was alternately doubting and aggressive. All his life he had felt poor, threatened. Even when he inherited a million at twenty-five he still felt the same and never rested till the one million was ten, diversified into property, of all kinds, houses, land, firms, and for good measure a controlling interest in silver mines far away. He worked hard and keenly. In ugly northern offices by sour canals and slag heaps. Many of his fellow peers were equally rich but like tired kings they treated it all as not really theirs, not property at all, more a job, a role and very fixed. Many of them indeed went so far as to have no idea what they possessed let alone how it was run, or not run. The wonder is that such weak and ineffective men could still be in possession of so much more than they needed when for more than a hundred years millions of others had had less than was vital. Perhaps it was their very ineffectiveness, even in some cases their simple goodwill, which had secured their immunity. And yet the world was changing in the way that it was changing, and when such men as Hitler, Stalin and Mussolini were in the ascendant it was difficult for some who were in authority to look upon such gentle sheep without casting, momentarily, a preferential glance at this other untypical peer who knew exactly what he controlled, exactly what was profitable and what wasn't. One or two such Juggernauts might with impunity be carried by the system, and even in return do some hushed-up, unrecognised carrying of the system, but not more than one or two. Which is not to deny that open despotism did exist on Lord Bewick's estate. There had been a killing, not it's true of a human being, but on one celebrated occasion of a labrador dog with which he lost his temper. Not surprising that war should have made him a Minister without his ever having made a speech or even once attending the House of Lords. A Ministry, in the new circumstances, had fallen into his hands without his even reaching out for it, and after six months in office he had already streamlined the stockpiling, delivery and rationing of fuel so that out of a heap of severed red tape emerged something workable. Nine headlines out of ten saluted him, the tenth suggested that his success was based on piracy—from other departments, led by men who were either more considerate of the needs of others or less accustomed to the uninhibited use of power, to say nothing of 'special' power—and special contacts, dating from schooldays on the one hand, and grass root work in industry on the other.

Yet this mogul of the moment sat on the silk bedspread in tears. . . .

Bertrand's experience was that you got *what you wanted.* But he was superstitious and lately his life had seemed to totter under a curse. His wife had died. Young. 'Without reason.' Then the fiasco of 'unecessary' war, and Peter choosing to follow a handful of butchers and bakers who had plenty to gain by bravery into the R.A.F., Peter, who had so much more to live for than a bakery and so little to gain by valour inspired by a month's carefully planned publicity called 'the Battle of Britain' which in the R.A.F. itself had already paled to nothing compared to the mortality rate in Wellingtons and other obsolete aircraft which were currently being shot down in droves over the German coast. Had Peter gone into the army he would have had some measure of control over his postings; in the R.A.F. he would be at the mercy of chairborne strangers, rule of thumb allocations to bombers, fighters of Coastal Command. Only too easily could he envisage a situation, quite soon, when Peter would be *out of reach*, condemned to an anonymous death in a cockpit that could just as well have been filled by someone else—not Peter Crowle, who should be kept for after-the-war should such a period ever emerge in meaningful form; just as Raymond Asquith, Patrick Shaw-Stewart should have been kept alive for the twenties.

There might then have been no slump! So Bertrand thought—and chewed his lip—a habit he had. To-day he had hurt it.

After his talk with Peter, he had spoken to the director of an Insurance Company, a lawyer, the family doctor (Peter had once had pneumonia), rung up the senior medical officer at the Air Ministry and finally extracted a promise from the

Minister himself that Peter would be considered for a vacancy as an instructor in Canada if he showed ability during his training. He was exhausted and looked round him with a sense of alienation at this permanent suite. He had chosen the third floor because it was said to be high enough to escape the worst of blast but not so high as to suffer from a direct hit, unless the bomb swung in from the side in which case it would probably rebound on to the street and explode there. . . . Where was she? Oh where was she? He knew it wouldn't be the first time, he knew he must always accept the possibility, though she swore in his ear after the Registry Office, like a child at a Christmas party, promised she never would, never, never. He was getting old. He had cried then and he was crying again now. More than ever.

'Nobody loves me,' he thought.

His hand strayed to the receiver and he asked for a Whitehall number, then for an extension, then for 'Lewson.'

'How is it?' he said.

'It's done, m'lord.'

He rang off, feeling better; then the telephone rang and it was Poppy.

'Poppy,' he claimed, his voice a discord, half threatening, half pleading.

Then her voice—like that of a whipper-in after losing a hound.

'Darling? Look—Fog again.' Her deep voice with its exciting timbre was never more clipped than when she was lying, nor more querulous, as though *she* were the aggrieved party.

'Where are you?' he said.

'*En route*,' she said. 'I took the wrong turning at Stamford. I'll be late . . . O.K.?'

Up at her old hunting haunts! Who was it this time?

He checked with the exchange. The call came from a place

called Boddington. He had them tell him where that was. Miles off. He bit the side of one finger for a bit and then went to his club where he played bridge, lost and shouted. There was an Alert and a few bombs. Heavy with brandy and cigar smoke he walked back to the Dorchester and found the double room still empty. Then he went to his own room. She wouldn't let him sleep beside her because he snored.

An *Evening Standard* lay on the floor: Kharkov in flames.

Everything that evening seemed to Lord Bewick to be crumbling. Even his emotional blue chips, Peter and Poppy, had slumped to an imitation of nothing. Soon the Germans might be here. Winston himself had said so, according to Chinks. They would confiscate everything.

Bert's thoughts gripped then on his 'last card,' gripped on it like a row of oily hands from a torpedoed crew. He actually dreamed about it—an ordinary tweed jacket, and inside it his child, the one who still loved him, Tim, arriving in America.

'Good,' he said in his alcoholic drowsiness.

The relief, which then showed in his face, would have been touching had there been anyone to see it.

5

Time-for-chapel was the more conspicuous for the lack of tolling bells—a sound reserved for invasion. Boys swept by seizing books, slamming doors, bumping each other—the great black, tail-coated tide of which Tim now was no longer part. When they came out he would not be here, so some called to him, slapped him on the back, congratulating him without conviction on his escape. Suddenly they had all vanished from the house and silence was a frame. With no picture. He went to a passage window and saw the arch of school-yard swallow the last hurrying figures, some jumping over the rubble which still lay scattered from the bomb damage to Upper School. Then he got a glimpse of Peter arriving typically at the last moment like royalty, unhurried. A vague blob of pain took shape in his mind. He was anxious for some sort of reassurance and the only person able to help him seemed now to be that tall, handsome receding figure there, the King of Eton really, who with every step became more of a complete stranger; or was that really what he had always been?

A last view of his housemaster was easier.

G. K. Saunders limped about a bit holding his pipe like an emblem and once picked up a paper-weight as though it were a lump of prejudice in himself. And replaced it. He wasn't fluent.

'You may pick up some *fossils*,' he said giving the last word ambiguous emphasis.

'Yes, sir,' Tim said.

In the past Saunders had been careful not to show too much interest in Loxley's dinosaurs, twigging him occasionally on his capacity to memorise the Latin names of vanished monsters —and of nothing else.

'Perhaps in America,' he said, 'you will have better opportunities.'

Tim had already thought of this. 'With any luck I'll get to Split Mountain,' he said. 'I've always wanted to.'

Saunders had not expected ever to hear a confidence from this boy's lips. The experience, at the eleventh hour, was confusing. 'Oh . . .' he grated, 'is that your . . . Mecca?'

Tim had never heard of Mecca.

'How did they *perish*, these monsters of yours?' Saunders suddenly burst out, affecting a courteous curiosity. 'Is it known?'

'There are a number of theories, sir. I favour "racial senescence".'

Mr. Saunders looked at him uneasily. Tim came to his rescue.

'It's the idea, sir, that species go through various stages like the human body—i.e., childhood, maturity and old age; then they become extinct. *Coelophyis* was the infant dinosaur; *Criceratops* the aged grandfather. I suppose it *could* happen to Man.'

The dour singsong drawl of this boy with the face of an angelic devil fitted into none of Saunders's categories; still less his mulish tendency to scholarship, even enthusiasm, down a blind alley of dead bones.

'Ah, well. . . . We don't know everything, Loxley.'

Tim could only gaze, as he had so often before, unfocused, at the middle of Saunders's desk, croaking 'No, sir,' careful even at this safe date to sterilise his voice and manner in case he be charged with 'dumb insolence.'

Saunders bit on his empty pipe. Better finish.

'Good luck!' he said—and stuck out a hand.

Tim's feelings for his Housemaster were the feelings farmers have for a long drought. It had happened. One made jokes about it if possible.

He put out his hand. 'At least, Tim, I know this: it isn't *your* choice!'

Tim said: 'Actually, sir, I'm quite pleased to go!' Colour came to his cheeks.

'I see!'

And that was that.

Miss Marlow, a small, sharp woman who had reprimanded him severely his first term for signing himself 'Loxley,' fussed over his luggage. 'Well, Loxley, I hope you survive.'

She always spoke in a high chirpy voice, concisely and firmly as though there must be no misunderstanding about her position as a female among so many young men. She said she had cousins in America. Tim said he'd look up her cousins for her, 'absolutely on arrival, ma'am.' The rudeness was intended.

His manner always made her panicky. She had a last go.

'What'll they think of us over there,' she said jerking his coat down, 'when they see you, Loxley? Or are you going to brace up? Look at your hair. I don't know! Will you remember us? I hardly see why you should. Wardle will miss you.'

The maid in question was at hand; she disapproved, from the doorway, roundly of the whole plan: 'What they wantyer to go there for ah should like to know: you're better off here where ye've got Wardle and that broother of yours. What's 'e doin', lettin' you go!'

And she looked as though she had been rudely affronted. 'Soom people need their 'eads lookin' into!' she decided and her eyes became vivid. She too had met Tim's father—and his stepmother.

'Give us a kiss then, Mr. Loxley,' she said bravely. 'And coom back soon. Now get off. Sharp, before Wardle keeps yer.'

'Thanks!'

Tim's customary tone of sardonic, pitying superiority was useful in discouraging physical contact.

For him the only true safety was to be found in isolation—and the only thrills in theory. The real world which he affected to disdain in fact terrified him. Occasionally, here at Eton, a master had warmed to him, rather as some men do to a cold and beautiful woman, or firemen to a person on a ledge threatening suicide. Perhaps these friends of beautiful Tim felt challenged by some obscure call for love as well perhaps as by an opportunity to be as conspicuous themselves as the hypothetical victim. But so far the only help to which he responded had been from vanished dinosaurs—and tailors. Lately, he had become dress-conscious, a move perhaps in the direction of other people.

The first signs of this fastidiousness had begun in the area assigned to his books on palæontology and torture and spread when his plaster model of a baby *tyrannosaurus* emerging from the egg, had earned a perpetual clearing on the table. 'Whatever's that?' Miss Marlow had cried.

'What does it look like, ma'am?' he had replied in the tone of a courtier seeking exile.

'A little monster coming out of its egg.'

'You've got it in one, ma'am.'

He stowed it carefully away in tissue paper, intending to take it with him to America. At the end of deadly chapel every deadly day he latched on to the words 'As it was in the beginning' with a feeling of release, identifying the words vividly with this scene which he had depicted carefully with his own hands: the beginning.

Charlie on the stairs in his cockaded chauffeur's hat: 'There's the man,' he said. 'All set . . . ? Over the seas to Skye!'

Tim smiled at last, his face opening mysteriously, his eyes taking sullen fire. Big Wardle noticed it.

'There!' she said.

Charlie had been on the scene as far back as Tim could remember. And Mrs. Charlie. Others came and went usually after some terrible scene. The victims usually turned pale in silence, then vanished. Tim had often wondered what magic protected Charlie and once when he raised the matter Peter had said, 'One day you'll guess,' a remark that stuck in Tim's mind and still nagged, when he saw Charlie, tall, solid, outspoken, sometimes insolent, ordering people about almost as confidently as Pa.

'On yer marks,' Charlie said, smacking his gloved hands together. 'Selling yer topper? Better give it to me t'keep the birds off the garden.'

Tim moved down the passage for the last time.

When they were in the Daimler he looked out on streets deserted except for one Roman Catholic going the other way. Harsh singing and organ tones were already audible from behind the sandbags and ancient stones. The pigeons careered about in a natural team.

So often in his life whether at home or at school, Tim had found himself as now, alone with Charlie, mucking about in the garage, fishing for pike, going to the flicks or even drinking Mrs. Charlie's dark brown tea which was the only tea he ever drank.

'Did you see Peter?' Tim said.

'I'm not 'ere for me 'ealth you know. Work to do. First you; then your parcel. Finish.'

'What parcel?'

'Oh Glory,' Charlie shook his head. 'I could tell you what flippin' parcel. Should have heard yer father. Think it was the crown jewels. Twelve-thirty, riverside entrance, ask for 'Ogg and open Sesame, show 'em this pass. I tell you I'll be thankful to be in uniform.'

He let this drop, disingenuously casual.

Tim said, '*What* uniform?'

'Army Service Corps—Tuesday,' he clicked his tongue succulently. 'Thankin' you! I told the wife. I said I'm sick of seeing the girls make eyes at all them old dug-outs just because they're wearin' a sack with badges. It's my turn. When I told your father—it was a Special! Shockin'! Know what he called it? "Damned nonsense"—joining up for King and country "damned nonsense." That's all from you, I said, for the duration!'

The idea of home without Charlie. . . .

Tim said, 'Well *hell!*'

'Won't make no difference to you—you'll be in America.'

For the first time then he felt as if he really *would* be in America. Even so, even if there were to be no holidays and he were going three thousand miles away then he still wanted to think of home as still *existing*. But Garston without Charlie and Mrs. Charlie was a weak idea. It slipped focus, blurred.

They were passing school-yard.

'Where were you when they dropped that lot?' Charlie said, with a glimmer of respect.

Tim turned and looked dully at the shambles of bricks and plaster.

'In bed.'

'Wait till they get Lord Crowle on their tails. Then they'll know it!'

Tim, watching the familiar buildings slipping away, the

Crimean cannon, the Virginia creeper on College Wall, the Wall itself where the Press sat on St. Andrew's Day, the odd beaks with basketed bicycles.

'Good-bye to the playing fields of Eton,' Charlie proclaimed. The car rose gently over the slope of Fifteen Arch bridge and came into sight of a French beak called Moulin bicycling along with his gown flying out behind him like black wings. Only two days ago Tim added some ink to that gown while Moulin bent over the shoulder of a boy in front. 'Inking Moulin' was a custom. The short-sightedness and fervour of the man prevented him from ever knowing that the true colour of his gown was by now indigo. As the Daimler pulled out and passed him, Tim looked down at the pinched face expecting recognition—a proof that he had been at Eton. Moulin saw but did not recognise him. For that matter, Moulin was already strange to Tim; suddenly irrelevant . . . And those old fives-courts, gleaming now in drizzle, looked like the bunkers of some disused industrial enterprise of which he had never had any experience.

'We got to step on it,' Charlie said. 'Riverside entrance twelve-thirty. And Mum's the password.'

'What's the parcel?' Tim said.

'I told you,' Charlie said. 'The Crown Jewels.'

6

Entering the Dorchester at four in the morning Poppy had managed to reach her bed without drawing more than a few unhappy grunts from her husband. Now she was sitting up in the autumn sunshine, spreading butter thinly on fairy toast. Beside her on the neighbouring pillow, flailing his tail from side to side in expectation lay her cream and apricot Pekingese, Duff, whom she occasionally fed with egg from the tip of her teaspoon.

Poppy was not beautiful, particularly when her face was covered as now with a grey patina of skin-food. Indeed she looked as though she were being treated for something desperate and total, like a rose-leaf matted with limewash. Yet even under these adverse conditions her low forehead, strong, hollow-cheeked face attracted a second look from the waiter who had brought in her breakfast. The secret perhaps lay in her eyes. They were large, deep brown and brimming with a look that was *hot*, *ruthless* and *deprived* like the eyes of a big animal in a circus, stranded on some absurd coloured box till the ringmaster snaps his whip. Yet who on earth could have been so cruel as to strand Poppy? The piles of jewellery on the dressing-table slung down anywhere and the silver mink, the clothes and stockings newly arrived from America, the late hour of a weekday, for a young person to be in bed at a time when most people had war-work—the illusion of peacetime—a prospect of bus tops and plane-trees in Hyde Park, the two white telephones, the egg-boxes on the floor and huge cubes of bright yellow butter each heavily embossed with a crown, the single letter B and *per ardua* suggesting something more non-committal than the motto of the R.A.F.—all seemed to repudiate the idea that anyone had been or ever could be cruel to Poppy. *How could they!* Those big brown bedroom-eyes appealed with a look of waif-like experience that lay too deep for her own or anyone else's knowledge, a look such as haunts the eyes of a London chimp wrapped in the *Daily Mirror* and December fog. It made sense some people claimed —to those who knew of her poor-relation childhood. These saw her now more as an exile than intruder. And others forgave her anything because she had rushed Bertrand's coffers and to his consternation scattered largesse in every direction. Even her enemies, and they included most women, would admit she had lit Garston up, started a racing stable, entertained all kinds of people such as her old Falstaffian uncle who had taught her chemin-de-fer if nothing else when she was eight, popular conductors, second-grade actors, columnists and all kinds of medical cranks who cured people strangely. Bertrand put up with it partly because for a time it made a change, but more because two or three of his financial and social rivals envied him the possession of Poppy, and if there was one thing which he had to have it was what others wanted. Sometimes she cost the earth—as when she managed to get a company of United States Rangers to give a display of special amphibious equipment on the lake with smoke shells and frogmen setting off charges under old punts. A boathouse had been blown up but unfortunately it had contained metal, some of which was scattered five hundred yards, one bit landing on the shoulder of a Free French officer. Also one of the frogmen got entangled in weeds and had to be restored to life artificially. There was an enquiry and for weeks people had to clear up all kinds of mess, legal as well as litter.

The American C.O. was moved and when his successor was killed at Anzio Poppy remarked, 'So I saved the other guy's life.' The takings were immense.

When Poppy presented the cheque (more than double the existing record) the Duchess head of the Red Cross thanked her thus: 'Perhaps any of us could have raised as much if we had done the kind of things you did. So Poppy. *Please* don't do it again!' And then of course Poppy, speechless, had *wept* in front of three heavily made-up ladies in armbands.

Of course she had soon collected herself, vowing that in future she'd drop something more solid than metal on anyone concerned with noble good works. And so on. This was the form, or part of it. Grooms admired her. On horseback she was Amazonian, tiny yet above all at home clamped across the very spine of the largest British tame animal. In India it would have been an elephant. But it was all rather a strain. Manly initiative might be a help in hooking a powerful man, but it was no help at all in living with him. No, it was no joke. You could see as much in her face already. Over the years Bertrand had become ruthless in demanding an infinity of heaven, here and now, in this world, using the whole of his equipment for pleasure, without hindrance from any code of morality and goaded to extremes by the combined weakness and disapproval of the people around him. Naturally he fell for Poppy, in her tight trousers, winning at cards, cheerfully iconoclastic, *impayable*, Poppy the roughshod rider. To some it appeared almost a *professional* marriage. But others who imagined they remembered 'a better Bert,' in the day when he was married to a woman who had never undermined their view of themselves, deplored the new association even to the point of cold-shouldering Poppy. That of course was all she needed in the way of provocation. She made sure of him. Got him to the Registry Office after running his vast household for three years of her early twenties. Her two children by a previous marriage lived upstairs at Garston. And still did. But lately the rifts which many had seen from the start had developed into a whole spider's web of cracks. The relationship went on. People wondered why. They loved each other: after a fashion.

When the connecting door opened with a luxurious *lisp*, Bertrand, pasha-like in silk dressing-gown, was smiling so broadly and instantly (as for a photograph) that one gold-capped canine showed clear as the spot on a Brahmin's forehead.

There could be no question about the smile: it was besotted.

'H'lo, H'lo,' said Poppy to the toast and then with mockery, 'Feeling a little calmer!' (she almost clipped it to 'commer').

He came close and she turned to feed Duff with the tip of her teaspoon.

'Aren't you cold, little girl?' he said and he pulled up a white mohair shawl that had slipped from one of her bare shoulders. In the course of this operation his heavy hand, which had a patch of long black hair on the back and more along the fingers, began to caress her bare flesh. She was not surprised because she knew of old that the words 'little girl' pronounced in a certain tone were usually prelude to this. But patience was not her strong suit. She sniffed crudely, and asked what had been hit last night in London. Then she answered herself:

'They got Whitehall, the maid said.'

He sat on the edge of the bed. 'You'll have the hot tea all over your lovely big feet,' she said in a technical tone.

He raised her hand, still holding the knife, to his thick lips and coarse moustache. She felt moisture and heat from his mouth and nostrils as well as stubble. But by not looking she kept calm.

'Your little breasts are cold,' he said, lowering his voice.

'My little breasts are minding their own little business,' she said. 'Now get off the bed before we all end up on the floor.'

'Let's end up on the floor,' he murmured in a low succulent voice.

Duff barked once, the very klaxon of jealousy.

'You see!' Poppy laughed. 'You've upset him.'

Bertrand did not like animals. In fact until he started having Poppy to live with him, he had hardly ever noticed them except as quarry, and then only briefly when he pulled the trigger. Now they were often brought to his notice as the objects of a consideration which Poppy seldom showed to human beings least of all to himself. Even her two small daughters were never caressed and held close to Poppy's face and bosom as this Peke Duff was. Nor were their wishes debated in a loud partisan tone. As those of this Peke were.

Bertrand looked blankly at the dog whose snoring face always smelt of stale snot—no disqualification this, from sleeping on the very pillow from which his own head had been exiled. For *snoring*. With Poppy he was always out of his depth —while wondering whether there was any depth to be out of.

'Don't look at him like that,' Poppy said. 'You'll upset him.'

She made herself laugh, a relief which he could not share. He lowered his lips again to her hand. 'Shall I put the tray away?' he said.

'Look, darling,' she implored. 'You don't really want it. Relax. It works. We know it does. Be like Duff. He just does it when he *really* feels like it . . . don't you, Sonny Boy?'

The arrival between the dog's front paws of her firm, warm brown bare arm immediately provoked it to a lively, semi-sexual agitation. He had very little else to do. 'Woops,' she said. 'I spoke too soon.'

Bertrand was angry.

The next moment Duff was on the floor, oblivious of how he got there.

'Don't you *ever* do that again,' Poppy whispered.

He slipped down her nightdress. She slipped it—up again.

'I got in at three,' she said.

Duff returned and got a little cream.

'What's the matter?' she demanded. 'Peter!'

He got up and said: 'Where were you last night, duckie . . . I waited up.'

His manner had changed.

'You got my message,' she said.

'Fog,' he said dubiously. 'And then the raid.' He loved her courage. 'Were you in the raid?' He wanted to hear 'Yes.' It might have brought him back to the bed.

Instead, she ate. She was wise to him.

He walked about a bit. His face had darkened.

'In future,' he said, 'I'd like you to do the journey by train.'

A morose look thickened in her eyes. Something further happened to his face too.

She said: 'I came because you wanted me.'

'I wanted to discuss my plans for Tim.'

'Well, *here I am*,' she pleaded.

'I wanted to discuss them last night.'

'I couldn't leave the hospital.'

'Cosgrave said you left after breakfast.'

'For Newcastle. The Red Cross stores.'

He looked at her, wanting to believe her. She noticed it.

'I *swear*, darling. That Florence Nightingale was on about my uniform again. She said it was a "bad example to the younger nurses." '

'But you're the Commandant!' he said unwillingly. He did not wish to be diverted.

'She said to me, "You're just Lady Bewick!" '

'Wah?' he barked.

He always breathed deeply from the stomach as though slightly out of breath. People put this down to his great weight but it may also have been due to the perpetually obsessed nature of his thoughts. Thinking like a dreamer, perhaps he breathed like one too. Deeply.

'The Matron,' she went on but he heard very little, picked the outside of one nostril with a hefty thumbnail. Again he barked 'Wah?' and with great difficulty switched from his own silent speech to loudly finishing her interruption of his thoughts for himself.

'I'll have a word with the Director of Medical Services. What did she object to?'

'My belt of cart-horse medallions . . . The soldiers adore it.'

He found a trophy with his thumbnail, checked it; went up and down, up and down. A fundamental principle had been threatened. She was into him.

'Wasshername . . . again,' he muttered.

'Codrington.'

'Codrington.' He halted, searching the name for danger, nobility, kinship to power, possibly, being a nurse, to Royalty.

Poppy said, 'What happened about the R.A.F.?'

'Tim will be here at twelve. He's going with you to Liverpool.'

'So you've done it. Are you right . . . ?' She did not wish to go to Liverpool.

Bertrand barked, 'Wah? There's nothing to stop them . . . *nothing*. Chinks saw Winston yesterday.'

Poppy took time to grasp his meaning, then she murmured: 'Goh'—liquidating the final consonant in marvelling horror. She could never resist the sensational.

Her eyes drifted out of focus, seeing Germans in Kent.

'That's not what he said on the wireless,' she objected.

Bertrand said: 'The less mouths to feed the better!'

She laughed.

'The whole object,' Lord Bewick explained tersely,'is to remove the children of the nation's leaders so they can't be used as hostages.'

Poppy was taken aback. She had never thought of that.

'But thousands have gone,' she protested.

'They couldn't just send the children of prominent people. There would have been protests.'

Poppy looked mulish. She refused to believe the Germans were as near as all that. She would have got up if she had. Nor did she believe that Bert was merely removing a potential hostage.

He continued, now, to inform her.

'The Dominions have offered to take twenty thousand children. The Government have encouraged parents to accept.' He was reciting—most uncharacteristically, and this made his tone aggressive.

'And have they?' Poppy said.

'Wah?' She repeated the question. He spoke contemptuously: 'In three weeks the offer has been twice over-subscribed.'

'Is that all?'

'All,' he shouted.

She said, 'When ten thousand people have been killed in air-raids, that's nothing—it's probably the number of people who'd like to get rid of their children anyway.'

This suggestion of many secret Herods missed him.

He continued his recitation, the fugue of his self-justification: 'The Americans have offered asylum to as many again—free. We ought to send our children away. It's the patriotic thing to do.'

This was not Bert. This was someone else. She looked like a water diviner in trouble: 'So Tim's got a vacancy,' she said dryly.

He said: 'I arranged it privately through the Children's

Overseas Reception Board. Tim's lucky.' His tone changed, became a little bit genuine, reluctant. 'He's in with a whole lot of 18b people. On the *Uganda*: waiters, Italians, ice-cream makers, cooks and German butchers. Safe as houses. Big ship. Recognisable silhouette. The U-boat people know. Hands off . . . Wah?'

'Have you sent them a little line . . . a little outline.' Her voice trembled with sarcasm.

Still he didn't hear.

'What sort of children are being sent?' she said.

'Six to seventeen.'

'I mean from what sort of homes.'

Bertrand was not a sociologist.

'It's here . . .' He clawed out a bit of paper.

Poppy glanced at it.

'Middle-class homes,' she said.

'It's his only chance.'

Poppy turned to Duff. 'Here, little boy,' and she offered the tip of the silver teaspoon.

Bertrand said: 'The Government has asked people to do it privately if they can.'

Never before had she heard him offer excuses for what he was doing.

Liverpool in November! Her face hardened.

She said, 'This isn't the first time he's been called away in mid term!'

She drawled the last word because even while speaking she lost the courage of sustaining what she had started. And she added, 'Never mind,' looking away, from him, as though she hadn't spoken. 'Little Man, Little Toughy,' she said to her Peke. 'It's time we got up!'

'What d'you mean?' Bert whispered.

'. . . Well, is it?' she said at last.

He looked at her. She had to say something. She kept on

with the special voice to make it all less meant, lighter: 'His prep. school . . . November? Was it not? . . . Five years ago.'

Never before had she even mentioned his wife's death to him. 'You told me yourself . . .' she pleaded. 'You had him up for the funer-awl. Isn't that right?'

'What are you talking about now?' he whispered.

'Wal . . .' she said, 'he's kinda been kicked around. Now he's getting exiled.'

It was not usual for Poppy to call up a child's past in explanation or defence of its present. 'Bleating,' she called it usually. In the present instance, however, she wished blindly, like an animal, to chew her tether: punish Bert for having it in his power to make her go to Liverpool, the very name of which filled her with misty, fishy, ugly apprehensions. He sensed this and forgetting her insinuations said: 'Why I want you to take Tim to Liverpool is to look after him—and his coat.'

'*Coat!* . . .' she said.

Bert took a few more obsessed steps.

'I've had it made by the MI6 people, same as for the agents we drop behind the enemy lines.' He was speaking thickly. 'I've put a little pocket-money in the lining . . .'

Her eyes flicked up to his face, alert. No wonder he had managed to rise above her mention of Tim's past.

'I wasn't going to tell you on the telephone . . .'

'I guess not.' Her mouth flickered humorously.

'Treasury regulations make everything impossible . . . Wagh?'

'I never said anything,' Poppy said and indeed she had lowered her voice, anxious to encourage confidence.

'He's got to have something . . . particularly if things went wrong here.'

'Sure,' she said. 'Sure. . . . Shoor!'

'As far as everyone else is concerned it's a life-jacket.'

Poppy laughed.

He looked at her.

The laugh lived on, though impaled by his eyes.

'What are you laughing at?' he said.

'Life-jacket's right!' She did something with her eyebrows which tightened up her features. 'Go on.'

'You tell him on board and not before. That's why I'm sending you.'

The phrase 'I'm sending you' did something to Poppy, not something new, but something additional. Her cast of countenance became more mulish.

Bertrand proceeded: 'Till then you'll be responsible for it. And the jewels inside it.'

'*Jewels* . . .' She felt a bit put out, deprived. 'Where is it?' she said.

'At the War Office. Charlie picks it up at twelve-thirty, brings it here with Tim, in time for lunch. You sign for it.'

'*Sign? From Charlie?*'

'It will be accompanied.'

For a moment there was no sound in the room except his footsteps.

'How valuable?' she murmured.

Bertrand did a turn or two. This was a moment he had foreseen but not decided on.

At last he said: 'About a quarter of a million. . . . About.'

Like a sceptic who has persevered at a boring seance and at last seen a ghost, Poppy looked suddenly blank with shock.

'Wal, Wal . . .' she said. And felt suddenly submissive.

7

Any journey for Tim, through the nondescript suburbs from Eton to London felt as though it ought to be happy, taking him to freedom. But this one was different. This, so to speak, was not dawn but an alarm in the middle of night.

In Acton he saw glass scattered all over the road like chips of ice and rows of windows, gaping black like broken cobwebs in an autumn morning hedge.

This was his first visit to London since the blitz in May. Traffic was sparse like a Sunday morning in peacetime. They came to more damage and then to a sight of Hyde Park. The railings had gone! Tim stared at the naked edge with a feeling of awe. Those high black spears of iron through which the grey nannies and the valanced prams had paraded year after year had always seemed set for ever. It was as though evolution had accelerated to such a pitch as to become a *visible phenomenon.*

Charlie said they'd have the stoppings out of their teeth before it was over.

'That's one from last night,' he added.

A house lay open to the eye, like a doll's house, showing the changes in wall-paper, from floor to floor and a fireplace for birds to nest in. A man in a white helmet was blowing a whistle at children and a van was collecting bits.

Far away among spires the barrage balloons looked plump and golden as fruit in the pale autumn sun. A sense of occasion made him notice things. Yes, Tim wondered when he would see London again, and what it would look like then. Until this moment he hadn't noticed much difference in life. The news bulletins had been good entertainment, a perpetual thriller. Dorniers, etc., like dinosaurs provided interesting classification. On the whole he had eaten rather more than usual, particularly of things like chocolate, butter and eggs simply because they had been made to seem more desirable while remaining, for him, as usual available. He had had, to be sure, a meagre, labelled pot of his own sugar downstairs —but a drum of it from Jamaica in his cupboard upstairs.

Charlie drove with the steady deliberation of the professional chauffeur. Each turning-off was a little ritual: a look this way a look that and then a majestic assertion of his right to move across the grain of the traffic, turning the steering-wheel solemnly, as though there was much more in even the simplest aspects of driving than most people like to pretend. Now they had entered Whitehall where the buildings were almost buried in sandbags and protected by triple barriers of concertina wire. Sentry-boxes with eye-holes and zebra fringes stood by doorways, and bored soldiers with fixed bayonets, occasionally coming to attention and saluting when recognised mufti went in or out. Charlie knew his way. Tim stared about him interested in the men's weapons, the curved magazine of a Bren gun, the squat length of some strange rifle; the new shape of women, buttoned into brown with bulging calves. It seemed to him perfectly natural that he should be driving into the very nerve-centre of Britain's war effort and that on one occasion the car should be saluted. There was nothing new about this sort of thing. Even before the war when he went to see Newcastle United, he had always gone straight to the Manager's box after a journey rather like this, and on those occasions the spike-helmeted police had also saluted, and the Manager or his representative had met him at the door to take him up the naked stone stairs to a room with carpets. Tim raised his hand in jaunty acknowledgment of a sentry and complained to Charlie about the bloody awful time it took to pick up one parcel. Finally they came to a barrier where it said '*No cars beyond this point.*' But Charlie produced several bits of paper. A sergeant came up slowly and looked at each slowly as though it would take more than a pass to pass him. Finally he took all the documents away and after five minutes a face appeared at a window and looked at Charlie and the car. Tim got out complaining. A pale-faced woman appeared, beside the man in the window, and looked at Tim for several seconds as though a good long look might be a great help to believing. Then all these faces disappeared and an officer came down, signalled the car on another twenty-five yards and asked Charlie to follow him.

'What is all this?' Tim said.

Then Charlie was back with a young corporal carrying a parcel.

'Better sit between us in front,' Charlie said and this the corporal did, holding the parcel on his knee.

'What's that?' Tim said when they were on the move.

The peak of the corporal's hat, pressed close to his nose, gave his eyes a far-away look as though something had come for ever between him and other people.

'It's a parcel, in'nit mate?' Charlie said.

'Ai,' the soldier said. Even his voice seemed to be partly on loan.

'Well, what's inside it?' Tim said.

The soldier stared ahead as though being inspected.

'He'll learn,' Charlie said to the soldier.

A vestige of a smile appeared on the corporal's spotty face.

The commissionaire at the Dorchester door was surprised at the people in the front seat, and opened the back door too as though something better had better come out. Disappointed he went away. Corporals with parcels should go to the back. Nor did he recognise Tim.

''Orse ficed Pouf,' Charlie said.

'Who?' Tim said.

'Is this where you fall out?' Charlie said to the corporal.

'Lady Bake, please,' the corporal said, and clung to the parcel, like a rugby forward.

'I mean it's careless, in'nit?' Charlie said. 'Expect the 'Orse Guards to come cloppin' on be'oind. O.K. then, Mr. Tim. Take 'im up will you. See yer.'

8

A lot of money, like beauty, has its own laws—and its own exemption from laws. And so for Poppy, who liked exemption, this coat was quite refreshing. She simply lay there, after Bertrand had gone, with a vision of it—one hand near her mouth and the other inert on the *Daily Mail*.

How she longed to ring up Jakey and tell him! Nothing ever really existed for her unless she could share it. That was why she couldn't and wouldn't put up with loneliness. Bertrand as a Minister didn't understand her needs; just as Jakey didn't understand the fastidiousness of her physical appetite—and it's unpredictability even to herself. Her blue moons! Last night she had made him suffer . . . *Every* night she made him suffer.

He enjoys it, she consoled herself. He enjoys anything to do with me, even suffering; and she looked sideways at the nearest of the white telephones, looked at it as might a child at its sweets—or a junkie at his needle.

She was neither quite lying nor sitting up, a position which made her neck look broken, an illusion which may have helped to discourage Bertrand's lust. The grease, too, must have helped.

How she stared at the telephone. Deferring pleasure simply to make it more acute.

Needless to say she soon lifted the receiver and dialled a

number. Her face became hangdog while the number rang. Then she said 'Jakey!' fast, hard and intimate while her eyes lately so inturned and morose, kindled with a vision, as though there, six foot away, the man she had spoken to . . . or rather cried out to had obediently leapt into sight. Then she said 'Darling!' conclusively: it being enough that he should be there, alive and available.

Then it began: a woman with an issue of words; at first bomb queries. Then she told him about every minute since they separated eleven hours ago. Duff had been sick in the night and she'd had a headache, Bertrand had been adamant: there was no escape: she had to go to Liverpool that very day. And Tim was going. 'Poor little blighter,' she said. 'He'd better have someone.'

Then she said bluntly: 'But what about you. Can you make it?'

The answer was implicit in her tone. Even so it took time in coming. She heard out his sibilant hesitations, his voice, like a fly in the pane.

'But you've got batteries in the north,' she said.

He talked but her eyes gradually lightened like those of a too-fond parent. He concealed his servitude by making it seem reasonable. He asked to be 'put in the picture.'

'God,' she said. 'Wait till you hear!'

'I don't want to wait,' came the voice. She looked at the doors. Her mouth flickered as she thought of the coat. She said, 'Peter has won.'

'So Tim's being pulled into reserve . . .'

'Yupp.'

'Does he know about us.'

'No.'

'Then how can we meet?'

'You're stationed up north. And you're a friend. You've even been to Garston . . .'

The voice at the other end seemed to have perished.

'Hallo?' she said.

'O.K.,' he said wearily. 'What hotel?'

'The Alhambra . . .'

Jakey said he would go to the Officers' Club.

She protested but he too was adamant. She sulked—said there wasn't much point in him coming unless he stayed in the same hotel. He replied that other things apart, he doubted if he would get in. She finally mocked him: Where there was a will there was a way.

He was completely silent as though she were having a fit which it was kindness to ignore.

'Know what's the matter with you?' she said.

He encouraged her to guess.

'Ever since I told you about Bert and his private detectives you've been scared stiff.'

'Is that it?' he said.

Poppy made a faint flatulent noise with her lips and looked sad. She decided to give in. 'Waaal,' she drawled, spinning him out, keeping him there. 'How will you do it—the Hamlyn Toob?'

His silence admonished her. Every day the papers ran news of people fined or even imprisoned for 'careless talk.' But she was not ashamed. A friend had told her the War Office had issued the Hamlyn Tube simply because the proper equipment was in desperately short supply, and any equipment was thought to be better than none if it kept people occupied.

'What do you know about it?' he said at last.

'A little Toobydoob,' Poppy said pretending she had merely mentioned a toothpaste, then suddenly serious, 'What does it matter mentioning an old plumber's pipe with two monocles in the middle . . . Winnie the Pooh's latest fantasy? He gets his fantasies in the loo. No, *honestly*, he does: I used to—when I was six. But I didn't have little guys like you to run around trying to stick them on to guns for me.'

'He's doing a great job, Poppy.'

'Of course he is. But don't kowtow to every little idea he has on the loo.'

'You're impossible.' Jakey's voice sounded almost estranged.

'It's all of *you* who are impossible. You go around like a lot of egg-bound hens with long faces and guns made of wood, taking four inches of tepid water in your baths and Hamlyn tubes in your stockbroker's bag expecting the Germans to be impressed. Why d'you think Haw-Haw's such a raving success? Because he's taken over the thing we believe we're good at: laughing at ourselves. God! *Admit* you've got two bodkins and a stinkbomb between the lot of you and start from there. Bert saw Pooh yesterday and all the little Christopher Robins are having kittens. Why d'you think Tim's going?'

'Churchill's against the children going,' the voice said acidly.

'You needn't tell *me* that, darling . . .'

And so on—and on, Bert said, Bert said, Chinks said . . . They said to her, she said to them . . . like five or six million women every day everywhere in Britain at garden gates, factory benches, shop counters, queues, sinks, stoves and wash-tubs—words too fast to be thought streamed from her, all with a mounting insinuation of scandal, sensation and chaos, a death wish for the shell of banality which even in war disappointed her wherever she looked. Perhaps it was she who should have believed in, perhaps even invented the exotic and useless Hamlyn Tube; no, as the voice in the distance knew well, Poppy when not in bed, or telephoning or entertaining, Poppy involved inescapably with a situation which demanded action and practicality such as a road smash lying in the path of her Hispano-Suiza Sports, or converting a large country house into a hospital, thrived and excelled—for at least a little while.

But she *was* in bed.

'Get up,' said the voice.

'Well, you know what you can do with that little tube of yours . . .'

Her laughter was ribald and somehow contemptuous.

'I'll visit you in gaol,' he said.

'You'll be a P.O.W. before I'm in gaol.'

This was too near the bone of probability. He blessed her and rang off.

She remained smiling as she replaced the receiver. The morning was better. She had cheered herself up, via Jakey.

And now she had company, quite apart from Duff, on whose body her hand found refuge, and whose tail flailed to and fro in hope.

'Give me a chance,' Poppy said to him, in a sober and personal tone, 'and I'll be right with you. We'll go chase something worth smelling. And you can bring your Hamlyn Toob!'

9

Alone in the choiring lift with the soldier and the lift-boy Tim fell to examining the parcel. The corporal clutched it so that his knuckles looked like peeled wood. Tim said, 'What the heck *is* that?'

The corporal didn't seem to hear.

A neat little 3 showed in the panel above the door and Tim led the way down the familiar corridor which reminded him of the Underground—a sort of carpeted Tube with lighted sofas and gladioli every so often instead of stations. As he walked he banged at the wall at rhythmic intervals with his knuckles, till he banged on No. 25 with the flat of his hand shouting 'Open up. This is the Gestapo. *Achtung!*'

There was Poppy, dressed as per usual, for the footlights.

He suffered a kiss as he passed her, jerking his thumb backward at the corporal, his face already set hard against the flirtatious teasing which was what he got from his step-mother.

'An object in rear,' he said. 'A fur coat for you from Stalin. With oceans of love, I'm sure.'

He looked round and saw Poppy signing a paper—and then another paper.

Then the corporal stepped back and saluted.

'Right—Fall out now, men,' Tim drawled imitating the O.T.C. Adjutant.

For a brief instant the eyes behind the pressed-down peak

deflected, as though on ball-bearings with a spot in the middle, each at a forty-five degree angle—and took in Tim.

For Poppy the remoteness of this military face amounted to a challenge. She offered hospitality. The corporal answered with a blush and increasingly glazed eyes. This irritated the Peke. After a long preliminary growl, he suddenly launched himself at the base of this immense cliff of alien matter and barked out shrill carillons of abuse. Poppy picked him up which turned his noise first into a love-snuffle then to a death-rattle of possessive growling. 'Aw,' she said, 'waazum a brave little soldier-guy,' and then looking merrily at the discipline she had tried to destroy, she said, 'Could you kill a German?'

The corporal's fear crystallised into a vigorous salute; and he went.

Tim said. 'You didn't have much luck there, did you?'

'One day they'll lose the key for him or the spring will break. Well, what about it, pleased to be going West?'

She searched his face, disguising her curiosity and fear of involvement with mockery.

He got up and trudged off, past her.

'You lucky thing,' she claimed.

'Where are my books?'

Tim hated this building. Poppy's Commandant hat was lying on a chair. He picked it up. During a raid on Newcastle she had organised a sing-song in a crowded canteen when the doors were blocked by debris: his father had won the D.S.O. in the First War; Peter would soon be in a Spitfire. He was going to America. 'What's that joke about the Dorchester?' he said.

'What joke?'

'That the German pilots have orders not to bomb it.'

'That!' she said contemptuously.

'Where's the point.'

'I suppose because there are people like Mr. Sam Glickstein living in it.'

'Who's he?'

'Just a guy.'

'Well, I don't get it,' Tim said. 'You and Pa are here, aren't you?'

'Yes. We're here. Now and again.'

He flung the hat down.

'Where are my fossils?'

'Where you left them.'

'What's inside that parcel?'

'A liddle coat,' she said, 'to keep a liddle guy warm.' She picked it up and squeezed it suggestively, tenderly.

'It isn't a dog,' he said.

She held the thing to her like a baby, her long mouth curling, and her dark eyes feasting on the face she could work on as certainly as upon many others, much older.

'*Would* you mind!' he protested.

She came close and put her knuckles against his face dragging the back of her fingers across his cheek till she reached his ear which she tweeked.

'A real warm liddle coat which Mother Poppy's going to keep safe till you're right on board.'

'If it *is* a coat for me, then why the hell did it come from the War Ministry?'

'Because it's a life-belt as well,' she said. 'It'll keep you afloat when you're torpedoed. For the seagulls to sit on.'

'You're a scream,' he said.

He flung away, wandered through the flat with great swinging steps looking for anything that might interest him or remind him of some previous occasion when he had been here. But there was nothing, except his *Palæontology in Europe* and a great pile of magazines under the eggs which Poppy had brought up from the country—American comics, and editions of *Life* with pictures of war, blown up so they covered whole pages, close-ups of corpses and black-shawled women weeping —and distant aircraft like blurred smoking crosses falling through pale tufts of ack-ack. He got stuck into them, leafing over the pages, impetuously and not reading much, waiting, occasionally speaking through the open intervening door—saying where was Pa, what was the form, when was their train, which was the Cubitt and when was it arranged. Poppy's answers were soon as absent-minded as the questions and both voices had the character of soliloquy. Then Poppy came in with a cowboy type belt and a sort of sombrero and bangles on her wrists like gold handcuffs that had separated. Perhaps in this attire she felt she lived up to the pugnacity if not the austerity of the moment.

'Christ!' Tim said.

'Like it?' she said, looking down and snuggling into herself.

'No.'

'Too bad. Look, darling,' she said in her sudden-serious voice which always had to be abnormally serious. 'I've *sworn* . . .' and there followed a long account of the oath she had given apparently months ago to two men with whom she used to hunt and who were about to be parachuted into the Balkans, that she would lunch with them the day before they jumped. That day (apparently it was common knowledge) had come. What was she to do? Let them down—or let him down. Or would he like to join them . . . ?

Her tone anticipated, to the point of dictating, his answer. So there was no need to wait for it. So, she went on, she had ordered him lunch 'in the other room.' Meanwhile, here was a five-pound note—and she flipped it on to the sofa: Maxy's Amusement Arcade in the Edgware Road was still open. 'You can play with the pop-guns to your heart's content.'

If there was one person in the world who could not

embarrass him about his recreations it was Poppy. In fact this was one of their bonds. But he stared apathetically at the note, the gossamer parchment covered with squirly black writing like a legal document. It was a lot even for him.

'And what are *you* going to do?'

'I told you.'

'But afterwards?'

'Come back here.'

'With one of your four-footed lovers!'

She pretended to go for him with her long red-toothed hands gaping like bloody jaws.

'Keep away,' he bellowed in his half-broken voice and rising with a rolled-up *Life* like a truncheon.

She took his wrists. She was wiry as a monkey.

'God you're weak,' she said, forcing him back.

A strange injected look came into Tim's eyes. 'Look!' she crowed. 'Look at this. Boiled macaroni,' and with a final shove she sent him on to the sofa where he remained in a heap, looking at her strangely.

'How the hell d'you know I *don't* want to come with you?' he said.

She was surprised.

'Well, come on then. Only don't hang around.'

She stood at the door and looked at her hospital-sized wrist-watch, her one sartorial concession to current events.

'Coming?' she snapped.

'I'm not *that* mad,' he said.

'Wise guy. Knows what he likes.'

'What's Charlie doing?' he shouted after her.

'Taking Pop to Chartwell,' she called.

She paused a moment. 'O.K.? . . . Then back soon.'

10

Two Tommies were bent over a plastic pistol peering carefully down the barrel. A sharp snap and the figure of Hitler on a bicycle sloped back from the parapet of the Siegfried Line. Washing remained pegged in the foreground.

Tim witnessed the achievement while a voice like melted Celluloid oozed over him. '*There'll be blue birds over, the white cliffs of Dover . . .*'

He loitered on past kicks in glass enclosures. Then another tune: '*I don't want to set the world on fiy-ah.*' It was as though the war itself were a musical. Tim peered into a football bagatelle machine with coloured lights. War had changed the Garston one to this; Garston to a hospital. If he was home now he wouldn't find anyone he knew, except Mrs. Charlie. His room was a linen-store (they said), but the pigeon loft in the garage had been got ready for him. The idea had appealed to him. There would have been storage space. He had always enjoyed himself in the garage. Now he would never sleep in a pigeon loft. His fossils were in the cellar. He let fly a great many silver balls. Then ran out of coins. There was a man with hair like patent leather drifting about between the machines as though he owned them so Tim asked him if he could change five pounds. The man looked at him in a way that made Tim want to be with Poppy. Or with Charlie. But the money was forthcoming, grimy notes and a weight of coins. He moved on.

Tried here and there, moving with feet that swung like pendulums.

The crane with the three-fingered grip responded approximately to his manipulation until the grip hung directly over the prize mouth-organ embedded in coloured balls. Then he lowered away till the steel finger straddled the bright instrument. Now—*clasp*. He twisted the handle sharply and the three arms came together enclosing a corner of the mouth-organ, tilted it. For a moment it seemed possible the thing would come away, drop on to the ramp and reach his hands, outside the case. But when he began lifting, it slipped out and the imitation of great power collapsed into a reality of none. A coloured ball did however stay improbably in the crane's grasp and reached him through the hole. In spite of coming out of a glass case it was covered with smuts, but felt as though it might be edible. He put it away in his pocket, and got down to the next toy with the next coin, using more strength than was necessary.

A woman with a jaunty air and an ill-looking painted face appeared beside him: 'Having fun?' she said.

Tim felt a cold clutch, a small crane's grasp in the pit of his stomach and moved away. But she followed.

'Like me to join you, darling?' she said. 'Why not 'ave a go. You'd get a prize for once!'

'That wouldn't be orl 'e'd get,' a voice said.

Who had spoken? Several bodies, back turned, were within earshot. Someone laughed and two airguns went off almost together. Snaps of elastic. Tim moved away. There was soiled paper underfoot and a legend 'What the butler saw.'

'C'mon then,' the woman said, still following.

Laughter welled up out of the screening music.

Tim pushed his way out into the street. Terrified. Disgusted.

The man who had changed his fiver was sucking a toothpick and looking at him. Then this man smiled, and cocked his head at him, backwards towards the airguns snapping and the mushy voice still yearning. Tim moved quickly—away, on down the Edgware Road, stopping at shop windows. Huge cards: 3/11 crossed out, for 2/11. He saw a clock and thought—they're just coming out of school. He could almost hear the tinny double-chime of the school clock and feel the momentum, now that he had left, of the geared life, the routine, the shelter of having a place, a reputation, yes, even his reputation. . . . It had made him Loxley, sometimes Tim. Now . . .

The sound of the woman's voice stuck to him like something foul and humiliating.

Boris Karloff in *Dracula* beckoned with green eyes and long nails from shadowy forests, along with a short called *Naked in Paris*. He went over to look. Often the picture outside let you down; because inside the girls weren't as naked as that; or they didn't move; though there had been Hedy Lamarr in *Ecstase* . . . Flicking over so fast you never even knew what you'd missed. He didn't care. It was disgusting.

There was one outside. She sat in front of a mirror so you got the best of both worlds: the world in front and the world behind.

Tim stared like a man watching a trick he had often heard about—say rope-lifting. Something inconceivable . . .

His eyebrows raised suddenly—the mannerism which periodically altered his expression from precise wary conjecture to the very opposite—blankness, receptivity.

The breasts seemed to him enormous, eyed like submarine monsters, coming at him. He felt weak and sweaty. The bottom was magnificent like *Tyrannosaurus*. Heady God. Supposing there had been some sort of crane, which by manipulating a handle, you bring the grip above the *reality* of *that* and then embrace it with three arms . . . Better than two!

Tim paid 2/6 to a woman who gave up knitting to make the slot eject a ticket. Her expression was almost blind with boredom and the event brought her eyes up quickly, past him, she too stretched her eyebrows refocused, taking note of time, not looking at him.

In the dark, alone. He looked sideways once to make sure that woman hadn't followed him. It was as though she had planted something in him and had come to get it back.

Again aircraft like far crosses through smudges, twisting then suddenly blossoming into black bloom of smoke and going downwards, pictures of bombs falling like shoals of fish, and the patchy flickering of their arrival, like sparks on a tram rail, then again the smoke and throughout the whole performance a steady roar of motors punctuated by explosions. Tim sucked Maltesers and some American candy he'd found in the flat.

A voice was pressing, sustained, 'heroic': Somewhere in England—Land Girls planting potatoes. Somewhere in the North Pole—War comes to the Penguins. Then ice and a voice saying, 'The still point of the turning world.' The phrase excited Tim as though it had something to do with him personally. He didn't know what was the 'still point,' but he felt it was right. The snow-fields didn't need comment, nor the glaciers. He himself became quite still all over; got a sort of shiver looking at the expanse as though God had walked over his grave. White, out of sight in every direction. He might never have been born. 'A land without frontiers,' the voice said. He had never been born.

The world is an extinct star, he thought, waiting for the amœba.

Twentieth Century-Fox . . . the old searchlights, fanfare and pillars, the crescendo . . . He put in a Malteser; a castle tower, a scream, kettle-drums, Boris Karloff loomed as fast as an oncoming train—they were off.

It was O.K. But the Paris stuff was deadly. Not a glimpse. Someone's underwear on a line and a hand putting it up.

II

Bertrand came in at four and found the suite empty and the door open. He called Poppy's name . . . then Tim's. Among the egg-boxes and butter lay a parcel which he scrutinised, lifted, pinched and suddenly tore open, literally clawing the expected garment from its paper-covering. Then he began saying things to himself and to Poppy while he pinched all round the edges of the coat. Finally he threw it down to lift the telephone, jiggling the bridge of the receiver.

'Where's Lady Bewick?' he barked. He got hold of someone who had seen her go out but this person did not know Tim by sight. The head waiter was got and he got another waiter who told Lord Bewick he'd taken up lunch on a tray for a boy but the boy hadn't been in. He had taken it up three times, finally at two-thirty.

Bertrand paced up and down the suite occasionally peering through the curtains at the street below. He was actually doing this when Poppy came in behind him.

'Wella, wella, well,' she said breezily. 'Home is the warrior,' and she put down a number of parcels and fancy boxes. In her coat was an orchid, her eyes were still laughing with the momentum of two hours' hilarity. 'Where's junior?' Then Bertrand's face caught the light and she saw it. 'What's the matter?' she said quickly and softly.

The expression 'speechless with rage' is seldom true. It was now. In the end he had to *act*—simply to make up for the words that wouldn't come.

He picked the coat up and put it down on the table in front of her and then pointed at the door which was as open now as it had been when he came in. At last he came on the air, with a sort of preliminary choking sound as though his circuit, after a long short and some sparking, was now complete again: 'I told you,' he said thickly. 'I told you. But you left it on the table with the door open!'

'Now don't . . .' she groaned but getting back her haunted look on the instant, 'just *listen*: I left the thing with Tim. I gave it to him!'

'*You mean you told him?*'

She closed her eyes and walked away.

'I'm not going to say another word unless you . . . *cut it out*. Just . . . just take a cold sponge and sponge yourself. Sponge your head.' She walked away from him, taking off her white gloves and chucking them down, and walking with her stocky aggressive walk to the flowers which she punched a bit this way and that. Some were sagging in the fetid central heating. She didn't blame them: she touched her own head.

'What d'you expect me to do? Take a wardrobe out to lunch?'

It was a brave show, a brisk volley from rifles at massed panzers. Soon it was all over: he *burst*, raved, battered her with sheer sound. Did she realise what was in the coat? Did she know what a sum like that meant? Was she such a baby that she thought that sort of thing *fell from the sky*. Yes—her face said, mulishly and she looked away because another person stared out of the charming pasha of Ascot whose grey topper had often tilted forward at the King, before conversation: an old soul, a half-Jewish soul who knew, but could no longer say, that men had given their whole *lives*, their health, their talents for one *hundredth* of this, or that children had died horribly for the want of one hundred thousandth of it.

'*You little fool*,' he hissed. She walked away entirely then, into the bedroom. He followed. There was a little wrestling at the door which she was at least not so foolish as to attempt to win. By then she was in tears. *And so was he.*

'And where is Tim? Why didn't you keep him with you. It's his last day!'

'*Why send him at all?*' she said ferociously.

'Why . . . *Why . . . You ask why?*' He was demented.

'Don't go *on*,' she whispered, only just able to speak. 'Take him north yourself. Make him a rat.'

The very phrase that Peter had used! In a worse tone.

He screamed: '*Because the Germans may soon be—there—in that door!*' and he pointed, for good measure. It was certainly one of the places where they would stand and she looked at it accordingly.

'And where will you be?' she said almost inaudibly.

'I'm sending Tim to safety!' he hissed.

Poppy had thoughts which she did not dare express. Indeed, they were almost strangers to herself, though she admitted them now, thinking: he's sending Tim to set up shop in the States; to establish a beachhead of cash; because he didn't move quick enough last year and his money's all tied up in Britain; also to perpetuate himself, the name, the title, the whole religion of which the emblem was embroidered on his slippers, his gun, his linen, his silver, his car. 'B.' B B B B B. All right, she thought, B B all right, I'm helping, what more d'you want, but leave me alone now.

She had begun thinking of him as 'he.' Almost as 'it'—formerly at her disposal. Now not.

Who knows what prevented her saying some of this? Could it have been *sympathy, connivance?* No. She swore she soon *would* say it! Yes, soon, she promised herself, she would say that sort of thing. But she didn't. She was afraid.

'I've got a headache,' she muttered. 'You call me a fool: but what could be stupider than to shout as you've been shouting with the door open—and to treat the coat like you're treating it, *all the time*!'

This altered him. She had touched one of the controls. Already he had lost Peter. Been too violent.

'Please, darling,' he said, 'help me!'

'For God's sake!'

She closed her eyes.

'*But where's Tim?*' He opened his arms.

'Where does he always go? He's at a movie. He'll come back.'

She walked away and sat on the bed.

'Your train's at six,' he pleaded, following her, his voice beginning to rise again.

She lay down and spoke wetly in a whisper: 'He's all packed. . . . He knows.'

She turned her back to him. He stared and began to get pleasure from the sight of her shoulder-length brown hair full of reddish lights, the smallness of her body, her arm with its bracelet, freckled with the light of hot suns and much open air. Her position made her seem suddenly a young girl, far younger even than she was: a child, scolded, with her presents scattered round her and her dog unable to give her comfort. A little girl! His rage turned more and more to pity. Suddenly to lust. How could this seductive little Poppy be expected to understand what perils beset everything she valued most, and always had beset them since B.C. and for years before the war. He had struggled, made enemies because he had the courage to appear openly what others were secretly, in which she had encouraged him, hadn't she, so must bear him company now, mustn't she: 'Duckie,' he said sitting on the bed. 'Duckie . . . duckie . . . D'you still like Tarzan? . . . Just a little.'

This had been the name she gave him when she first saw him naked. Seldom since. He offered it now with a smile which revealed the gold-capped dog-tooth beneath his moustache and reached for her tight little bottom which he appreciated most in the trousers she usually wore at Garston.

But she moved as though pinched, away.

'Don't,' she pleaded through tears.

'Shall I join you, Duckie?' he begged.

'I've got the curse,' she said as crudely as possible.

A door banged, and she revived instantly, rolling over and saying: 'There, that's Tim: Your sinking fund!'

He didn't get it.

'The *Benares!*' she said.

To hear the name of this ship, sunk a month earlier in transit with a load of children on their way to Canada darkened the face of Bertrand to the colour of chocolate.

She had at least this much in common with a wife: she knew what would exasperate most.

Then he began. She pleaded, said Tim was next door, finally shouted: 'You haven't even said *Hallo* to him yet!'

But he wouldn't stop.

'The *Benares*.' He hissed. 'You and Peter talk about the *Benares*; neither of you know what you're talking about . . . You say "*Benares*"—you don't mention the bomb that fell a hundred yards from Tim, you know nothing . . . *nothing* of what may happen here soon . . . Do you . . . *Do* you . . .' He pointed at the door as though that same German soldier stood in it now. 'The *Benares*!' Strangely enough even while he poured out his torrent of certainty his large and formidable face was haunted by doubt, the kind which might there and then have driven him to open the door and tell Tim to go back to Eton. Poppy's mouth flickered in scorn.

'O.K., O.K.,' she murmured. 'He'll float. . . . But I repeat: hadn't you better say Hallo to him first?'

12

And Tim heard them at it.

He loitered away from the connecting-door swinging his feet into a sort of slow goose-step that helped pass time. It brought him to the coat. He stopped, looking down at it, wondering at the ragged way the paper was torn half off it.

The Peke was under a chair looking gun-shy.

'Duff,' he said, half to announce his presence and half in concern. 'What's the matter with you? . . . If you chew my life-belt I'll bounce you a few times against the ceiling!'

Then his father appeared, dog-tooth showing, eyes glistening, smiling hotly. 'Columbus!' Bertrand said. 'All set?' and he looked at the son who was not Peter . . . took Tim's arm high up and squeezed it standing close to him and inspecting his as though he had volunteered to become Peter, fly over and kill Hitler single-handed . . . 'Pleased . . . ?'

A sort of heat always came off his father, as from a furnace. It prevented Tim thinking.

Tim said, 'Where have you been, pray? Chartwell?'

'Yupp. Had a word with the great man.' The dog-tooth showed still in the broad smile. Tim felt vaguely uplifted, as though the side-effects should have been different.

'America was what you always wanted,' his father said. 'The Grand Canyon, monsters . . . priddy girls, pop corn, film stars: Galina. Maybe you'll see Galina again, what? Pleased? 'Course you're pleased. Galina.'

'Speak for yourself. Why do I need a life-belt?' Tim fixed his eyes on the coat with dislike.

He wanted to hate something. Something safe to hate, i.e. not Pa or Poppy.

'You're in convoy.'

'Then why a life-coat? What's the flap?'

'You're sorry to leave Eton,' his father stated firmly, moving away, and jingling change in his trouser pocket. 'Maybe you'll be back in a year.'

'Thanks.'

Silence fell and Tim looked round restlessly.

'Where's Auntie?'

'She's resting. She'll be right out. We've got a special tea for you. Bottle of pop!'

The tooth glowed again and Bertrand's eyes were hot with love—and insistence that what was happening was *right for Tim*. 'Good flick?'

'Average,' Tim said, and sat down heavily. Then he began whistling half a tune. He looked at his watch. It was only three twenty-five. He got up and fetched the pile of magazines as though his father were not present. He expected to be spoken to again but Lord Bewick went through—to telephone.

Tim was forced back on *Punch*: reading the captions to the jokes twice because he doubted they could be quite as wet as they seemed at first. But they were wetter, though it's true they were homely in the sense they evoked the world he knew, the long table in the morning room at Garston where every newspaper and periodical you could think of lay in regulated layers, each peeping above the other, until disturbed; soon rearranged by a footman who came in at half-time to feed the vast fire with a polished brass bucket, piling the silver-veined coal so high that the satin of the nearest cushions was almost too hot to touch and screens had to be put between, hour after deserted hour. *Punch* was part of the nameless feeling that had so often clamped down on his heart, to the sound of the latest tune, and the rattle of backgammon dice or coal in the polished scuttle, driving him at last to the happy smell of petrol, tools, activity and Charlie in the garage . . . To-day three *Punch* cavemen in skins were gazing up at a dragon flying over; one said to the other, 'That's one of ours.' Tim turned back to *Life*. At least it never failed to give you flesh —and blood: live flesh swelling and spilt blood dripping.

But even *Life* in some way failed him, seemed a part of advertisement, causing him to turn the pages quickly, like someone looking for something specific, and not finding it, ever.

13

The waiters wheeled in the high-tea. Bertrand went over to it with the tips of both hands in the pockets of his maroon velvet smoking jacket. He had ordered champagne of a certain year. So he checked. Then he looked and saw lobsters separated by a mosaic of peas and tiny potato-cubes made into a message '*Bon voyage*, Tim.'

'What's this?' he barked. He smiled so that all his teeth showed. 'Who did this?' He radiated hot approval, enveloping the waiters, the chef, the hotel manager.

'For No. 25,' one of them said.

Poppy swept in tossing her hair back over one shoulder, revived, smiling triumphantly. 'A little message in peas from Henri . . . Like it?' and she pulled Tim towards the trolley. 'See! *Bon voyage*, Tim?'

The waiters fell back towards the door. All was explained.

Tim said, 'Who's Henri?'

Poppy said, 'A little guy whose wife makes my hats.'

Bertrand grunted and his smile dimmed.

'Is that real mayonnaise?' he said.

Poppy said, 'I gave Henri Garston eggs, American olive oil and vin de vinaigre; he got the lobsters himself from Oban. The partridges come from Garston. Any complaints?'

Bertrand smiled and put a great arm round Poppy's waist, drawing her close; grinning at Tim as though they ought perhaps to start by eating her, so delicious, so unfailingly fresh and surprising she always managed to be. Then he looked down at her as though posing on the *Queen Mary*.

'Ducky,' he said. 'Can I have a kiss?'

Tim decided to concentrate on lobster, but heard the kiss.

'Do you love me again?' said his father.

'Have a heart,' Tim said. 'I'm eating.'

Poppy said, 'You're putting him off his Last Supper.'

'Thanks.'

'Where's the coat?' Bertrand said suddenly.

'Wherever you left it.' she said briskly.

'But where is it?' They could both see the torn paper which was indeed where they'd both last seen it.

'Well, *you*'ve been in here,' Poppy accused almost laughing. Bertrand's face turned into a hooked-nosed devil mask like the villain in a traditional Japanese play. And his voice was all bubbly again, deeper, softer than normal.

'Where is it?'

Poppy lifted a cushion. 'Not there . . .'

'An above average lobster,' Tim said.

'It must be here,' Poppy said.

'What?' said Tim, lost in the sheer white, firm flesh, and real mayonnaise.

'Your little life-belt seems to have taken a little walk—right —out—of—the room.'

Tim never heard a word. Ecstasy, however brief, is single-minded. Besides when he did focus his father kneeling to look under the sofa, the spectacle did not connect with echoes of 'coat,' least of all his coat; nor indeed with anything.

Poppy also had never seen Bertrand upside down before. She began laughing.

Tim said, 'Have you *quite* taken leave of your senses?'

Bertrand looked up at her, with blood still suffusing and swelling out the end of him that was normally uppermost.

No mask had ever achieved such an effect. Poppy's fear of him merely increased her desire to laugh. She raised the back of her hand to her mouth and snored helplessly, the very negative of a guffaw.

The moment passed. Cool as a cucumber she said: 'It's here . . . I know it's *some*where.'

They walked about as though playing a game.

'Has *everyone*,' said Tim turning round, 'gone completely bonkers?'

'Where's your new coat, Tim?' Bertrand said.

'Well, I'm sitting on it, for Christ's sake.'

Poppy's laughter then came out. Bert looked at her. She held both hands towards his face as though to ward off a blow. 'Stop,' she said. 'I've stopped. Look!'

Tim said: 'I don't get this coat. We fetch it from the Houses of Parliament and I'm told it's a life-jacket but when I tried it on just now I felt like a knight in armour. I could hardly walk, let alone swim.'

'Have you ever tried on a proper lifeboat life-jacket?' his father said. 'They weigh twenty pounds.'

'Well why not get me a boat while you're about it?'

Bertrand undid the champagne and the cork hit the ceiling. Tim cheered and held out his glass. 'Pour!' he commanded.

Tim gulped but his father held up his class ceremoniously. 'Think of us sometimes when you're over there,' he said—and then to Poppy: 'Tim!' Suddenly his hot, dark eyes filled with tears. A child, he thought, my child going away! Alexandra's Tim!

'Tim,' Poppy said and lowered her eyes.

'He'll never write,' Bertrand said.

'He never does anyway,' Poppy said.

After two glasses Bert felt different. A few moments ago with his head under the sofa he had felt suddenly impotent.

Now he felt omnipotent: not even Hitler outside the country, nor regimentation within, could prevent that sense of himself which agreed with him. He was Garston. That immense Palladian architrave which surmounted the steps towering above the arriving visitors as the door of the temple of Apollo towers above the visitor to Baalbek with enough clearance for two giraffes placed one on top of the other was for Bertrand a central feeling so that when he saw other men he thought of them vaguely in terms of their front doors. Therefore, compared to himself, as ants.

'Poppy. The only girl!' he soon said.

She made the door live. And she made it unique.

If another man did have as big a front door (as some did) then it didn't count unless occasionally the King went through it: the King, Douglas Fairbanks, the Prime Minister and winter squads of Dukes taking off their mittens. All these conditions were fulfilled for his own vast door. In war and peace. Death eventually might seem to threaten the whole position. But not really. If you built strong enough you went on—in your children, your property, your power. Nothing could stop you. Nothing! Peter was a fool.

Free French in London; Free British in New York. The telephone buzzed discreetly: Charlie was at the door.

'Here we go!' Poppy said, like a bomber pilot.

'Attaboy,' Bertrand said.

Tim had had two glasses of champagne. He laughed weakly.

'I suppose you know I'm drunk,' he said with a touch of malice.

There was a moment's silence as there is in a play when one of the actors forgets his part.

Poppy stared at him uncertain of his meaning and then looked away laughing briefly.

'Well, I am,' Tim said roughly, and remained seated.

'Come on,' his father said. 'You've both got a train to catch.'

Poppy looked strangely at her stepson as she did at Duff when he wanted water in a foyer or a train.

Then Tim got up and said, 'I can stand.'

He looked round the suite and thought: Even this will still be here to-morrow . . . Then he was aware of his coat being lifted from behind him by his father and carried into the bedroom where his suitcase was lying open.

'In here,' his father said to Poppy. 'In this, blue one, is that clear?'

'Do my eyes deceive me?' Tim said. 'Or is that my father packing?'

Poppy had to make an effort not to laugh. She took over the business of putting the coat away though she couldn't manage this without saying something which Tim couldn't hear and which his father disregarded.

'MIND MY DINOSAUR,' he had occasion to yell.

'Mind his dinosaur.'

Tim said: 'Don't ships *provide* life-jackets?'

'Not the best make,' Bertrand said.

Of course. All his life he had eaten something, done something, gone somewhere different for that same reason. It made sense. The coat was after all merely the as per usual.

But the excursion was not! Most definitely not. Again he got the funny feeling of unreality, not quite dream, nor yet quite memory which reminded him of being woken up to see a taxi on fire, in Cadogan Square, when he was four; as a treat.

14

At the station entrance Lord Bewick shouted 'Porter' into crowded gloom. Soldiers stooping forward from the weight of kitbags and bulging packs stared curiously like savages at a grounded aeroplane.

Bertrand had sent a message to the station-master. But the bystanders did not know this. So how were they to understand his tone? They didn't. But some of them had come to know the voices of drill sergeants and so looked vaguely over their shoulders in the other direction expecting someone to come hurrying; which someone did: a man with gold braid round his cap which he touched, obsequiously, while behind him came a porter actually *running*.

Lord Bewick then indicated which cases were to go in the van and which in the compartment.

They all set off into ghostly space with the station-master and Lord Bewick leading the way, then the luggage, then Poppy carrying Duff and her white kid vanity bag, finally Tim slouching beside Charlie.

'You'll be back soon,' Charlie said.

Inside there were pale shafted pools of light slanted here and there revealing a figure struck in some posture of somnolent apathy or blunted expectation. Raw yellow wood, scaffolding, dirty sand. A platform was closed and beyond it, high, a huge hole in the roof through which Tim could see the remains of daylight to the west, fringed with a jagged edge of twisted iron and cracked glass.

A distant rhythmic thudding and the limited movement of many people, none of whom seemed to be quite sure in which direction they should be going, made it like a vast ballroom in which a dull dance continued though the lights had fused.

'They had one here!' Poppy said. She had the same tone for bombs, as for operations: Visceral and ghoulish.

Charlie said: 'Not as bad as Paddington.' This one would do for Poppy. 'Tell those Yankee-doodles to send up a pop-gun,' she told Tim.

Tim could hear his father barking at the station-master far in front, and then the station-master's explanations.

Their footsteps clattered and Tim thought they were like cattle being driven along a new road.

Suddenly the sirens started their low crescendo.

'I was waiting for it,' Poppy laughed. 'Plenty of glass here, little man!'

She wrapped a rug round her dog's face and body.

The sirens reached the required note then sank, then rose till they got into the stride of creepy undulation. It was almost the same noise that Tim had heard that afternoon from the bowels of Castle Dracula.

'What happens now?' Poppy called to Bertrand with a touch of derision. 'Back to Eton?'

They passed faces looking up under lights. There had been enough raids lately. Some figures were moving away towards the Underground. A loud-speaker crackled and heads turned vaguely listening and then turning again as though expecting someone nearby to explain: now a deliberate voice embarked on a long, scarcely audible message: travellers should go to their trains, others were advised to make use of the shelter or proceed quietly to the Underground. People for Liverpool should board the train.

'I don't know why your old man didn't let us motor,' Poppy complained.

Increased uneasiness came over Tim whenever she opened her mouth in public.

'Is your journey really necessary,' she read out, laughing.

'Would you *kindly* stow your gab,' he said.

She accused him of being 'windy.' They moved on along a queue, past the barrier, which for them was no barrier.

The train was packed, people bulged out whenever a door was opened.

'Aren't we just a shade late,' Tim said.

The station-master led them to a window where they could see two first-class seats which two large labels had kept empty. (There were four officers in the compartment, staring vacantly, waiting for whatever was going to happen next.) But how to reach the seats?

'Better say good-bye here,' Poppy said tersely, speaking louder because of so many voices, engines and loud-speakers.

'Stay outside,' Bertrand said. 'There's no hurry.'

'Then put something on the seats. You never know.'

A whistle blew. 'Better get in.'

People in the corridor looked curiously at the woman and the boy struggling through flesh to reach their reserved seats and Tim felt unwilling to meet their eyes. In fact as soon as he sat down in the corner he stared out through the anti-blast patchwork of sticky paper which covered the window. He touched it. The porter came with the luggage and the station-master appeared at the window. People in the corridor and the officers were staring openly or stealing quick looks at them.

Then Bertrand began to ooze and shove his way through the packed corridor, which even empty would have fitted him as closely as a gunbarrel fits a projectile.

When he reached the door he looked up at the rack.

'All present and correct,' he said and reached out an

enormous arm so that his overcoat dangled across the face of one of the officers.

'He's put the wrong case in here,' he suddenly said in a strangled voice.

'It doesn't *matter*,' Poppy whispered. But it was too late. He was going back through the corridor like a Rugby League forward while people pressed themselves this way or that. No word of apology not even at peak moments of compression. Once on the platform he yelled 'Porter.' The loudness and passion sounded mad. People looked as though a bomb had dropped. Tim saw Charlie begin running and the station-master walk after him waving and looking worried. An officer beside Poppy put down his newspaper and considered them as though they were an exercise without troops.

Poppy groaned and stared at Tim with wide, wide eyes that asked him a question. But what question? Tim shrugged violently and angrily. He put out one hand and toyed with the filthy ash-tray. Then he took out his knife. Anyone might have wondered if Poppy were inviting him to laugh, or cry since her own expression gave a small lead in both directions.

He said, 'I should be somewhat disturbed by this commotion did I not know the *dramatis personæ* were all barking anyway.'

The porter appeared outside with the other suitcase, protesting vigorously that it was too large for the rack when the rack was already full.

'Now!' Poppy said. 'Watch!' She said it really to the four officers. But they were watching already.

The door at the end of the corridor opened and cold air again enveloped ankles.

The porter's progress along the corridor was characterised by the clumsiness of revenge. If that was how they wanted it then that was how they should have it; from here on, apparently, he absolved himself of all consideration for man or beast. Duff did in fact let out a howl as he crossed over him. The officers, foreseeing the shape of things to come, began moving their legs and feet and looking helpfully and scientifically at the crammed rack.

'Which one is it then?' the porter said swiftly.

'That one,' said several voices, and Poppy began laughing.

'Don't bother. Just *pretend* you've changed it,' Poppy said to the porter. 'He'll never notice.'

The porter froze with the suitcase poised over several kneecaps. 'Wassat, madam?' he said harshly and stared at her as though this at last was the proof he needed and certificates of insanity could now be issued forthwith all round.

'Oh, nothing,' Poppy said.

'Nothing, is it?'

A whistle blew a kind of frantic morse code. One of the officers rose to help.

'This out and that in?' said the officer. The question was rhetorical: he and the porter fell to like navvies. But the rack was piled to the ceiling.

Tim tried to help but was unable even to get to his feet.

Bertrand appeared at the window, scrutinising the exchange, then he smiled charmingly so that his dog-tooth showed, and raised one large hand shoulder high and waggled the fingers, did the R.A.F. gesture thumbs up, then Winston's gesture, the V sign, then a sign asking them to part the window. The station-master came to his elbow and explained. Departure was imminent—and inevitable. Bertrand's face darkened and he moved out of sight. A moment later he could be heard coming up the corridor again, apologising. People muttered and then there was Bertrand again, in the doorway, cornering the porter who by now was ready to retreat to the van with the other suitcase which if it stayed here would have to lie on the floor where there was already insufficient room for feet. But he couldn't move because of Bertrand.

'God bless you, Tim,' Bertrand said throatily and held out both hands. Tim got up but owing to navigational difficulty said: 'What happens now?'

'Y'can say that again, lidy,' the porter said and put his cap farther back on his head.

'Sit on my knee,' Poppy said and pulled the porter, who was precariously balanced, towards her.

He collapsed looking round at her in amazement. Poppy laughed. One of the officers raised the *Daily Telegraph* as though unwilling to see more.

Bertrand reached right over and managed to apply his lips and whole moustache to the face of his son who received this experience, as he received others, as though it were all the same. Then Bertrand clawed at Poppy, reached her too round the porter.

Poppy made an effort, after the kiss, her voice changing to the tragedy Act V tone which was her only way of being even a little bit serious.

'Don't worry,' she said. 'Everything will be O.K.'

The whistle sounded again and the station-master appeared at the window. Bertrand retreated, followed by the porter, the soldiers squeezed forward, a child howled, the brakes wheezed. Then there was Bertrand making faces at the window, grinning fiercely, *willing* Tim across the Atlantic with the coat, *willing* his survival, Poppy's return without getting held up in any more fog and now again certain that everything would be all right.

'God!' Poppy whispered and she looked round the officers who with the one exception seemed to have no choice but be an audience. One smiled thinly; another withheld a smile; the others looked remote and sociological.

Tim saw Charlie appear behind his father's shoulder and raise a gloved hand. He responded.

His father placed the whole of his right palm against the window as though conferring something sacred and enduring on the train, on Tim, Poppy and the coat.

They moved, the hand thumped three times on the papered glass. The dog-tooth shone—like Sirius.

And that was that. Pain. The last of his father . . . the last of London—except for searchlights probing the clouds and crossing each other, lines of a luminous geometry, AB produced to BC cutting XY at O . . . no more of that. He felt numb, mad, seeing nothing really but Poppy's haunted face under the feeble cone of light, motionless now as a waxwork, not looking at him any more, looking out at the night, but obviously not really looking at anything. He wanted to ask a question but the question was so vast and complicated that he didn't even know what it was.

She faced him.

'O.K.?' she said mechanically.

'A new high in chaos,' he said.

She smiled—kindly.

She was thinking of Jakey.

'Look here,' he said. 'What the hell was all that about that suitcase. I'm not going to need a life-jacket between here and Liverpool, am I?'

The *Telegraph* came down, critically.

She said: 'It's got the eggs in. They get broken in the van.'

'*Eggs!* I thought . . .'

'Play a game,' she interrupted. 'Gibbets . . .'

He was insulted. While he was scorning her she wrote something on the back of the *Evening Standard*, and handed it over to him while he was still giving his opinion of 'Gibbets.'

He read: '*Don't talk about the case. I'll explain when we arrive.*'

He handed it back. She tore off the strip and crumpled it up.

He felt stranger than ever and from then on sat thinking about *that coat* . . . working back from his father's amazing performance at the station right back to Charlie disappearing into the War Office. The connection was obvious.

His spirits revived. Soon he was able to think of himself as being after all a bit like other people. Peter was going into the R.A.F., Poppy ran a hospital and his father ran almost everything, these officers round him were set in their roles; and he, even he, had a secret Coat, which came from behind concertina wire, sentry boxes.

Pop knew American senators . . . That was it: he was carrying something important to America!

Perhaps that was even why he was going . . .

A sudden unexpected exultation took hold of him; his eyes shone with bleak conviction and in the dozey hours that followed he slid easily into the role of Secret Agent, enduring the slights of men like his housemaster, for a Cause that was somewhat above the level of an Eton beak, thank you very much, G. K. Saunders and Miss Marlow in particular.

And there was some point!

After all.

15

The movement of the train made Poppy think of Jakey who would soon be leaving from the same platform, in the same direction. Her spirits rose too. She was free again and on her way to her lover. Meanwhile she had Tim, and the four officers, particularly Tim whose brooding, sensitive face had always stirred her as the faces of her own daughters did not. She looked at it now with the special pleasure of having it to herself. But Tim had gone to ground in one of his books. She turned to the officers and managed to provoke a debate with the two nearest on the phoneyness of some of the things that were being done, such as blacking-out the name of stations, 'all those boffins imagine a spy with a thick Hamburg accent in sun-glasses and a butterfly net.' At Crewe she put her head out of the window, sauced porters who responded well to the chance of repartee with a young woman in the dark. 'You see: "Crewe" they tell you: so what's the point? Besides if the Germans did come they'd know which was Liverpool better than the town clerk. It's time we stopped playing Red Indians . . .'

She spoke in a rapid querulous tone as though she were defending herself against some kind of accusation. But no one had accused her of anything though it was possible they soon would.

'Have a heart,' Tim said, putting his fingers in his ears, and only with difficulty, read. Great sums had been spent on his education but to date the influence of the printed word had come mainly from *Palæontology*, *A History of Torture Through the Ages*, and Bertie Wooster. The first two supplied the inner man, the third sketched briskly an identity which seemed vaguely possible; he was happier at Blandings than at Garston and the idea of a butler hero corresponded roughly with his own experience of Charlie. If such phenomena as his brother, father and stepmother were absent from the Blandings scene, then that, as far as he was concerned, was the essence of the holiday. But Wodehouse didn't reach the entrails. For that he required red-hot pincers, death by a thousand cuts, the Indian refinements of *Kittee* (a thing like a lemon-squeezer) and *Anundal* in the course of which you were tied, sometimes for days, in agonising positions (he was getting to it now). *Kittee* and *Anundal* like Dinosaurs *nourished* him . . . Poppy's conversation with assorted strangers set his teeth on edge.

If she *had* to talk, which presumably she did, then let her tell him the one and only thing he had the smallest desire to hear from her: the nature of his mission. And it was this thought which leapt out when someone at last said 'Liverpool.'

Now he would know! He snapped his book shut. 'About time too,' he said, and then, as soon as they were in the taxi, 'Let's have it.' But they had company.

'I heard the North West got it again,' Poppy called to the driver, proving earshot.

The driver made a scoffing sound, 'When you hear "North West" you can take it from me: that's us . . .' He spoke as though addressing a stupid wife and afterwards rolled his head a little, insulted.

'When it's London, it's London,' he went on, 'but when it's Liverpool it's the North West! Thut's how it is.'

'You got it bad!'

'You'd better list'n to Lord 'Aw-'aw.'

'I can't bear his drawl,' then turning to Tim. 'Worse than yours.'

Tim said: 'I'd sooner talk like Haw-Haw than sound like a whole Punch and Judy show.'

The driver said: 'What's it like your way?'

'London,' Poppy said. 'Got it last night. Night before Newcastle. They follow me round.'

'I wish they'd catch up,' Tim said.

'Every night here,' said the taxi-driver.

Poppy said: 'Hit—or miss?' This was an inquiry.

The driver hesitated like a card player. Then he said:

'Bit of both like,' as though laying down a small unimportant card.

'They got the post office, the power station, and the gas works beside us,' Poppy said. Three aces.

A tremor shook the back of the taxi-driver's head. He played fair.

'Coom they'll get the gas works 'ere,' he said, 'if we get too many visitors.'

Poppy laughed. And the man moved again. But she went on:

'Whitehall's flat, Churchill's kitchen is rubble.'

The taxi-driver let a long moment pass and then said, 'But 'e isn't!'

'Take a lot to flatten him,' Poppy said.

The driver let her have this.

'Where are we?' Tim said staring up at the succession of enormous silhouettes.

This was another opportunity for the driver . . . 'On the way to the hotel, Sonny.'

'Hell, Hull and Liverpool,' Poppy murmured. 'They can say that again.'

The driver heard. Regional and class distinctions had been softened by war but Poppy could have sharpened them up in Moscow—or cut across them in Buckingham Palace, a two-way faculty existing in her to a degree which seemed to prove the truth of the saying: opposites meet in their extremes.

The driver shifted as though in a draught.

Soon they drew up in front of a dimmed-out 'OPEN' from which a figure emerged and immediately vanished. Poppy looked at it. 'God!' she said. Courage to face danger or even a completely different kind of life came easily to her if it conferred prominence, or even rich experience. But this . . . this place promised merely bed-bugs and intimate noises through thin walls, trouble with a commercial traveller in the lift; malodorous plumbing. Things she had said Good-bye to for ever.

The driver opened the cab door, and grasping the suitcases got shot of the lot, putting them inside the hotel door and coming back for his fare. Disapproval radiated from him.

'You're lucky to get anything,' Poppy said, 'shooting your mouth off about what's been damaged. We might have been spies!'

Tim turned away as though from a riot. Then he heard them both talking, *laughing*, then Poppy's clipped steps as she marched briskly towards the swing-doors.

She went in like the police—and was amazed. It was O.K.

'Just waiting for Albert Consort and John Brown's cosy little Body.'

While she was signing the reception clerk handed her a telephone message from Cooks: it would not be necessary for Mr. Loxley to board ship to-morrow after all: the time of departure would be notified later and a Mr. Simpson would get in touch with Lady Bewick in the morning.

Poppy groaned and said: 'Britannia doesn't even rule the bath!'

'What?' Tim said.

While she was still shocked a man in a black suit and striped tie came and bowed to her: 'I'm sorry, Madam—no dogs are allowed in the hotel. But we have a kennel.'

Tim sloped off to sit in the lift with the luggage. He didn't want to hear a word of it; but he couldn't avoid it. Not that it lasted long.

Soon Poppy appeared with her vanity bag and Duff under her furry arm.

'I won,' she said.

'You don't say.'

The page inspected them as they went up.

The passages were vast, the fittings brown and heavy.

'A barrack,' Poppy said, 'for salesmen.'

Tim had never slept in a British provincial hotel before and Poppy's experience was limited to the Dorchester and Claridge's where she had spent one or two week-ends under an assumed name. Entering the unlocked room, she looked about her with dismay—at the dowdy wall-paper like a jungle on a monsoon evening, the massive furniture which seemed to have relied on sea-transport right up to the last hundred yards, long brocade fringes to the lights and plumbing which stood out into the middle of the room in the shape of a broad square basin which reminded Tim of the sinks in the old laundry at Garston, massive chinaware with splash-shields eight inches high and tall taps, each containing two or three pounds of metal, and underneath all an intestinal proliferation of pipes, both to and from the basin, all furnished again with taps, six inches from the floor labelled like their distant connections above, Hot and Cold. This convenience was such an encumbrance that it drew the attention even of people like themselves not normally interested in water-engineering.

Poppy peeled off her snow-white gloves while she appraised it. She could take bombs, she could wipe up vomit or fit a tube to the flaccid member of an incontinent old man in stale sheets—but she could not stand contact with what most would have regarded as luxury. She imagined she would have preferred a ditch.

'Jeepers,' she said to the page. 'Is this him or me?'

'You're together, Madam.'

'No,' said Poppy. 'We are not.'

The page explained she had been booked into the same room as the gentleman.

'Well, you can unbook us,' Tim said.

'We'll soon fix that!' Poppy said and went to the telephone. But Reception was adamant: Lord Bewick had booked them together. Besides, there was no other room available.

While the altercation developed Tim gave in to curiosity, unlocked the biggest case and took out the coat. He didn't like the purplish colour, nor the pattern.

The page stood at the door. Poppy's eyes drifted from her indignation to the coat and the way Tim was touching it in front of the page. 'O.K.,' she said to the boy. 'We'll stick it out. There's a war on . . .'

The page left and Poppy said, 'D'you have to make love to it in public?'

Tim felt the edges thick, wadded tight. Then he looked at the '*Utility*' mark, two sort of blocked-out Ds.

'Possibly *now*,' he said, 'you might come clean.'

Poppy said, 'It's got money in it . . . Your keep—in America.'

Tim was dismayed. The school fees—instead of a message to Roosevelt. He threw the thing down.

'It's just in case anything should happen here,' she said.

'Presumably gold,' he said.

'Never mind what it is.'

'Like hell,' he said. 'What about me?'

'What d'you mean?'

'Is it legal?'

'Don't worry about that, ducky.'

'Then why sew it into a coat?'

She turned away, hesitated and said:

'So you won't lose it!'

He looked at her and felt rage rising inside him. It was always the same. Terrific talk about telling the truth; and then terrific lies, all round. When you challenged them: silence, evasion.

'I want to know what happens at the Customs, if you *don't* mind.'

'I've told you: nothing. Now that'll do.' Poppy the governess always completed his bewilderment. Particularly when her severity was followed, as now, by a teasing look.

'*Why can't Pop send a cheque?*'

'Everything's frozen.'

'FROZEN?' he roared.

The financial and legal conversation that followed could have enlightened no one. Poppy, like Tim, had to see things before she believed them, perhaps even touch them. Frozen billions of sterling assets eluded her. Anyhow Tim required more than a Poppy to lead him where he did not want to go.

'In other words,' he said. 'You haven't a clue. But possibly you could tell me *How much*.'

'A few hundred pounds. Perhaps a thousand.'

'Crikey,' he said. But then he remembered his father's face when he first saw him coming out of Poppy's room, the scene at tea and at the station and the way Poppy had written the message on the newspaper so that no one would hear. It didn't make sense. Why make so much fuss when Poppy wore jewellery every day worth five times as much as that. No one said a word when she left it about, which she did, all the time. He pointed this out.

She said: 'The jewellery is insured.'

'Then why isn't this?'

There was still something missing.

She shut him up. But looked at him.

Animals were able to enlist her support for their slightest whim.

'Now what's biting you?' she said.

He didn't reply but loped away, fiddling with his knife. She followed him with her huge suggestive eyes, weighing up his possible displeasure and now inevitable presence against the arrival of her lover in the morning. How long might she not have to dovetail the requirements of this one with those of Jakey and herself. She knew Tim. There weren't many people who would have taken on what she had. Even Bertrand was scared of him, Bertrand and schoolmasters. In fact there were only three people living who could cope with him. Charlie, Mrs. Charlie and herself. And why? She felt a little pulse of heady power as she told herself the answer: she knew what he liked and gave it to him.

'You don't believe me,' she accused.

But he wouldn't speak. So, she thought: he doesn't believe it, as I said he wouldn't. Far better to tell him the truth!

Tim sat down and loosened the cork-screw from the main body of the knife.

As one who demanded nothing less than complete liberty without strings for herself, Poppy was quick to recognise serious frustration in others if that frustration were likely to prove in the smallest way inconvenient to herself. Alerted, she would try to forestall trouble by putting herself in the position of the person concerned, and suggest what to her would be a way out—often with the most ludicrous results, since people vary greatly in what they regard as a 'way out.' In the case of servants she relied simply on an increase of wages, money seeming to her the only certain way of being free, free from every ill in the world except death and accident, and even relatively free from these. This view had resulted in her employees enjoying riches, and leisure in proportion to their capacity to inconvenience her or (same thing usually) to their closeness to her person. Her lady's maid, for instance, had only to groan to get an extra £1 a week. The sky of course should have been the limit; in other words her method was a fairy tale. But Poppy of course had no time for fairy-tales. How lucky then that Bertrand's resources were in fact exactly like some fairy-tale purse, always full. The system had worked; become a habit. So now, when confronted with Tim's frown which promised a threat, in some obscure way, to her freedom to-morrow, and, worse, a more precise threat to his acceptance of the coat she decided to tell him *now* what in his place she would rejoice to know as soon as possible—how rich he was. Only then she felt, would he relax—and she be free.

And so she told him.

For a few moments he was silent, his face blank, visionary. Then he said. 'Is it mine?'

'It will be,' she said. 'Now get this. Your dough's in your coat and without your dough you'll be cleaning windows before you're eighteen. So hang on to your coat and don't talk about it.'

Tim was impressed by her tone—which was vibrant with the knowledge that she herself would have been unable to clean windows, except possibly as a reconnaissance.

He stared uneasily at her hot, rough eyes.

'Remember Mother Poppy's words: stick to that little old coat!' and she went on looking at him toughly as though she might take it away from him unless . . .

Unless what?

He got up sheepishly and touched the coat again. It was ghastly. An oik's coat.

'I can't wear a thing like that.'

'Believe me, you'll wear it to-morrow.'

The telephone rang and Poppy picked up the receiver. 'Bert!' she jerked, and Tim saw her face become careful and withdrawn. 'Yupp,' she said. 'Yupp . . . Okayee except they . . . or you put us in the same room, almost the same bed.' She looked at Tim beginning to laugh. He watched her moodily. 'So it *was* you! Safety hell. You might have consulted your wife before you made any incestuous arrangement. I've a good mind to ring up the police . . . *Of course* it's against the law.' She loved putting people in the wrong, particularly Bertrand. Her voice began to take off as it did in company and Tim had the feeling that everything she said as well as her scandalised tone were partly addressed to him. She even looked at him while speaking.

'You needn't think *I* want to be in here,' he interrupted.

'Ah,' Poppy cried, delighted. 'He says *he* doesn't want it either. We'll get a screen . . . I'll have to tuck him up . . .' She made herself laugh but Tim could hear his father's voice admonishing. Soon she was saying 'O.K. . . . O.K. . . .' in the low, restless grudging tone which always blighted her when he or indeed anyone asked her to do anything. 'Yupp, it's here right now, he's cuddling it . . .'

Then his father's voice, loud and insistent. She made protesting noises but couldn't force an entry. Suddenly she burst in: 'Suspicious? . . . You've already made him a sandwich-man. Advertising Jewels.'

Then there was shouting. Which she equalled. The reluctance of each to divulge over the open line what they were really talking about in direct terms or even what prompted their sharply different points of view made the row more chaotic and therefore rougher than usual.

'Oh, *for Christ's sake*,' Tim said, and flung the coat on a chair.

'Look . . .' Poppy crowed. 'You've made him throw it away!' and laughed silently but still covering the mouthpiece as she did so and shaking her head at Tim as though he were on her side. In the end it all blew over with Poppy promising she would never let the thing out of her sight. 'He can sleep on it . . .' Her huge brown eyes ogled Tim suggestively. 'Round his neck: Yupp . . . take it easy,' and then she seemed to make some sort of effort to drag her voice down from the heady heights of banter '. . . thinking of you too . . .' she said, then lower still, 'Yes. Love,' and made a kissing sound into the receiver and laid it down. 'God,' she said.

Tim said, 'What?'

'Nothing . . .' she hummed. 'No thing.'

Silence fell. Tim sat, bending forward fiddling with a morsel of sweet-paper:

'Where're the people I'm going with?' he said.

'They're joining the boat direct. Now bed. That's your side, this is mine. I'm going downstairs a moment. And I want you to be in bed like a good little boy by the time I get back,' she smirked and clapped her cupped palms like a severe governess, 'and if you're very good you'll get a good-night kiss, otherwise a hard slap on the boko.'

And she came slimly towards him. 'I've "got you" in here!' she threatened.

'You just try,' he said, staring at her intensely but feeling strange all over, his heart a turmoil of emotions.

She turned away to the door.

'Why are you going downstairs?'

'Haha,' she said, and disappeared.

Tim stared round at the unfamiliar room with its long brown curtains and heavy Victorian furniture. Poppy's make-up was already spread out on the dressing-table and the coat was lying where he had flung it. He looked at the walls and wondered what variety they had witnessed. Two people in a bedroom reminded him of his mother and father; not of Poppy and his father. 'I'll tuck you up!' she had said. The last time he had slept in the same room as a woman was with his Nanny. He was enraged.

He stared at her clothes, her nightdress which she had strewn on the bed. There was a boy called Fraser at Fison's who had been found in the bedroom of the Austrian cook. Both had been naked and both been sacked but Fraser had lived on in Tim's memory, even though he hadn't known him. Fraser, Tim thought, would probably have regarded this here as an opportunity.

But Fraser had gone off, into the world, as Peter would soon do. They would kill Germans . . . Tim slumped apathetically as he took off his shoes staring at the coat. He felt he wasn't just looking *at* it, but *through* it, at the events of the last twenty-four hours, right from the moment his name was called at Absence to the conversation he had just heard on the telephone and on from there, from now, to his departure to America: everything in terms of that common coat with a nondescript purplish pattern. How could Poppy be so sure the American Customs wouldn't search him? He remembered her face when she said, 'you needn't worry about *that*!' But *why* needn't he worry about it! He *did* worry about it. Poppy! Every time she opened her mouth she increased his ignorance. It was as though he had entered a maze of glass in which familiar faces were quite close but incommunicado and unattainable—in time and space. A few hours away were Peter, Fison, Miss Marlow, Charlie, his father and the Dorchester flat; there in Newcastle, quite close, was home, now a hospital, his room a cupboard, his things 'stored.' And in the other direction . . . what? Skyscrapers. He could hardly imagine anything except *skyscrapers*, and when he remembered his father's teasing promise of 'popcorn and priddy girls' he could call up no vision except the side of a breakfast cereal carton—and then shame, embarrassment, as though the whole female sex had no other function except to make him feel silly. As far as he was concerned the whole tribe could sink to the bottom of the sea and *good luck* to them.

His shoes fell with desolate thumps while his eyes remained fixed, unseeing, on the coat.

Where the hell has she gone, he thought and wished vaguely she would come back. She had been known to make sense, he decided, in a blue moon. Unlike some.

16

If sailors have a girl in every port, Poppy had a peer in every county. The advantages were enormous. Like a Rotarian or a Zionist official she could move far afield almost without expense and with every facility that money and influence can offer. Here, for instance, in Liverpool, the problem of fixing Tim up with fossils, billiards, dungeons or shooting while she enjoyed privacy with her lover seemed no problem at all: two telephone numbers of provincial palaces within thirty miles lay ready to hand in her bag. From these, in the past, she had attended Aintree; and one of the owners had even for a time come under her spell, presenting himself in her day-dreams as a possible mate.

But it transpired he was in Cairo, without even leaving behind him a major-domo to remember her. And the other owner was in London.

After this second refusal she experienced the thick heady feeling of frustration which sometimes got her into trouble in traffic, as when she was fined for having all four wheels on an Oxford Street pavement.

The call-box stank. She stood there wondering what to do. She didn't even know the number of Jakey's hostel. Suppose he never came . . . or something prevented him! Suppose the convoy didn't sail for a week. She felt desperate. He *must* come; and what's more she must find the means of a little privacy when he did.

Besides, she herself had no intention of sticking around the old Alhambra day in day out. Liverpool for her, like every other place she had ever been to, meant pleasure, and it was this which suddenly drove her mind back two years to the Irishman she had met at a training stables . . . Springfields, and from whom she had eventually bought a pony. Yes, Jimmy!—Jimmy Lennox, who sent her a Christmas card last year. Supposing he was still there . . . Soon the Springfields number was ringing and Poppy's mind was schooling with merry thoughts with which to revive brief acquaintance. Hadn't he said he would never forget her, even if he lost his memory? Her pessimism vanished and she waited eagerly for a voice. It came and was at once, obviously, the wrong kind of voice, old, bemused, caretaking. Springfields had closed down. Everyone had left. Then where had Jimmy Lennox gone, she asked. *Who?* And so on: apparently he wasn't known, but Mrs. Dowell might help. She did: she was even older, by the sound of her, but she knew Jimmy Lennox was staying in Light Street, next to the Madras Hotel, No. 42 . . . Telephone number? Poppy asked. The woman was amazed at the notion. Poppy took the address. God, she murmured as she came out into the air of the foyer. The outlook was bleak. She stood there blaming Bertrand. The war so far had been fun: adventure in a new get-up, more power than usual and enough professionalism in her management of Garston hospital to give her an unusual sense of weight (she had done six months first as a V.A.D. at Newcastle). But this sort of blank was unspeakable. She looked about her at the massive dowdiness of Victorian Liverpool, imagined tea-brokers with sideboards, do-gooders with millions and no humour, Quaker stockbrokers, and the colossal smugness of Victorian riches—as personified by one of her own great-grandfathers. Canals, steam and grime. Puritans. Yet she might be here for days.

The cheerful noise of a bar with its outside chance of a face she knew lured her to have a look. But at first glance the uniforms were not promising. No cavalry chain-mail or Brigade of Guards buttons in sets; and the accent of the voices that hung on the air was not her world. Still she walked right through, since there was an exit the far side.

In public, in the midst of strangers, Poppy looked like a high-class tart, a similarity which lay more in her expression than in her clothes; something brazen yet haunted, as though she suffered acutely from the very thing she courted—attention. Had she been a man her brisk 'chippy' manner might have passed almost imperceptibly for the common characteristic of men who are what she was, small. But in a woman it stood out—as did her jewellery and her gaudy clothes. And yet . . . one or two conversations flagged. Men's eyes picked her up, steadily. But she found nothing worth a reciprocal interest.

'What a dump,' she thought, and it occurred to her that Bertrand had sent her where he would never dream of staying himself, even in war-time. And so she felt justified in having Jakey.

In the doorway of 207 she was surprised to find darkness.

'Tim?' she inquired sharply.

No reply.

She thought she heard the level breathing of deep sleep so she turned on the mirror light and started to undress.

At the first rustle of clothing Tim opened his eyes like a sentry. But the strip-tease he had been waiting for never happened. Poppy undressed as though preparing to jump in and save her life: one moment she stood sheathed in clothes and tangled with ornaments, still promising him hours of careful, sinuous extrication; the next she was stripped to her goose flesh, marching across the room towards her nightdress, cupping her neat pear-shaped breasts briefly in the hands of her crossed arms. Instead of a dance of the Seven Veils it was to be once again like Hedy Lamarr in *Ecstase*: $\frac{1}{100}$ of a second exposure. His eyes sank weakly but fast to the fork of her legs, to the most exciting and conspicuous absence he had ever seen, the most haunting nothing. As in the Edgware Road, his spine felt sweaty and his head light: hair he could see, a little triangle. Frizzy. He was frightened, as frightened as when they had made the over-elevens dive at his private school, from the top springboard. Better if that delta had been much, much closer—or not there at all; better if *close as food*—or utterly and forever alien.

Suddenly she stopped in mid-floor and stared amazed at his open eyes. Her long mouth curled and she went on to her nightdress. 'Peeping Tim,' she laughed but a shade awkwardly as she tweaked it towards her and got into it. 'We hope you enjoyed yourself,' and she plumped down in the front of the mirror, attacking her hair with a stiff brush that made a violently harsh panting sound as she whisked it through the long strands. She was smiling faintly as she brushed.

Several times then she seemed on the point of saying something. Tim was glad she didn't. His anger had gone and he wanted her to behave as she was now, as though this were simply her room, where she always slept, and this night one of many similar ones, with him in bed before she was, and she sitting there, methodically preparing her body for rest. But he was not so pleased when she started on her face, slowing up suddenly as though dealing with a wound, first removing the old dressing and then gently applying the new, two layers of grease kneaded in with a circular, hypnotic movement. She could have done it in bed or walking about the room since it required no guidance but apparently she needed to look into her own eyes while she was doing it—her flattened fingers going round and round while those two dark eyes searched it seemed for something infinite inside themselves. And all the time she became more and more deathly in colour, more adhesive. In the end he couldn't stand it.

'Do you *always* embalm yourself before hitting the hay?'

'Go to sleep or I'll give you a little squirt of *Mon Pêche*!'

'Thanks a lot,' he said.

She worked away.

'Want it?' she mocked.

'Just you TRY,' he said, hoping she would.

'Right.'

There was a hollow cupping sound, like stage-hoofbeats, as she put on some pot lids.

She looked at him in the mirror, smiled and looked back over her shoulder. 'I'm on my way!' Her mouth flickered.

'You're going to get a little good night kiss,' she said. 'Momma's going to tuck you up . . .' She got up and walked across the room, self-conscious, jaunty, knowing well, with every step exactly what she was doing.

He watched her come, in silence; even when she put one hand on either side of his head and bent down so that her hair trailed across his face he still didn't move or say anything. Just when she seemed about to kiss him she laughed and tickled his neck. The movements of her nail gave him the feeling of a large crustacean proceeding down his back.

'Look,' he hissed, 'unless you want to come to a *really* sticky end somewhat before schedule . . .'

'Your voice is breaking,' she said.

'Yours has broken.'

'Peeping Tim,' she said with a note of aggression.

'When there's a single thing worth peeping at, I might peep. But not before.'

She gave him a little cuff across the side of the cheek. Tim erupted like a jack-in-the-box, wide awake, sat up, and as part of the same movement with all his strength and even while she was screaming for mercy caught her a full swinging slap high up on the thigh.

Her eyes filled with dumbfounded tears. 'What on *earth's* eating you? That hurt!'

'Good'—and he burrowed down into the bedclothes, as though alone in the room.

She said, 'Liddle man had a busy day. Overtired.'

Tim would have liked to beat her. How was he to know that many others had felt the same?

She got into bed and flicked out the light. There was silence except for a few late vehicles on the road outside. Both were very conscious of the other, lying so close in the dark. A long hoot came from the river, reminding them of the Atlantic, quite close, behind all the buildings.

'Good night, darling,' Poppy said suddenly in a bleak, passionless tone.

She had suddenly thought *he is going to America. Right away.*

But this effort of even a little sympathy exhausted her, introducing her, as it did, to the fringe of her own threatening wilderness. She turned back from that.

She turned away from him.

Tim also turned away, thinking of the body beside him, which he had cursed . . . then of the coat and his father. A great sense of desolation enveloped him. He wished he could have been in the pigeon loft at Garston with his books, tabulating bones and the pleasing shapes of the earliest locomotives. Alone—with the relief of sheer facts.

17

Big Wardle crashed through the door with a can of hot water at seven, using the noise of the whole operation to make sure he was awake, crowning it with a cry 'Seven o'clock, sir.' But it was a bus, not Wardle. Tim stirred and took stock of his surroundings: fug, the presence of another body and the smell of female unguents. Soon claustrophobia made him break with habit and get up before he had to.

While dressing, he stole a look at Poppy, who was lying uneasily, as though sleep had more problems than an exam.

Dawn, the same colour as her skin-tonic, filtered through the curtains and set a seal of ghastliness on a face now as strange to him as the thing he had never seen, a corpse. He wanted her to be so different that he went out gladly into the deserted passage, closing the door quietly as a thief. There he paused, thinking of the coat. Should he have put it on? He decided not.

A clock in an alcove said ten to eight. Downstairs, the porter was poring over a paper. Tim bought the *Mirror* for Jane. 'Coventry again last night,' said the porter.

'How many did we get?' said Tim. The old man who was called Fred Letter, sniffed, and looked over his spectacles like a schoolmaster getting the wrong answer.

'Is that all you think of, son?'

Tim shrugged him off and followed the signs to the dining-room, swinging his long legs and gazing ahead with an expression of restless criticism.

On the way was an immense window like that of a pre-war shop, and in front of it, for some reason—he paused. The window was quite out of keeping with the rest of the hotel. Through it Tim saw a vast area of what at first appeared to be nothing. He was not one for views but on this occasion found his eyes drawn outwards, perhaps because the window was something like a cinema screen, say at the Empire, Leicester Square, starring on this occasion, a few chimney pots, on the lower rim. Suddenly he realised he was looking at water . . . the sea perhaps, and at once the chimney pots took on the crazy semblance of distorted and swollen periscopes. He remembered yesterday's life-boat epic, and to-morrow's . . . Suddenly the mist seemed to coagulate in the middle . . . and took shape as a ship, gliding inwards apparently on air since it caused no ripple.

Tim went through. The dining-room was like an officers' mess with only here and there a sprinkling of civilians.

The nearest waitress, a woman in her late fifties, immediately favoured the lonely boy. Tim was not surprised. 'Possibly two kippers instead of one,' he suggested, 'might be allowed.'

She said she thought it might and forgave him his tone of voice on account of his broody blue eyes.

'And I'd like marmalade.'

'Well, you can pretend it's marmalade.'

Later when she put the little portion down beside him she whispered in his ear, 'It *is* marmalade,' and gave him a nudge.

Again—he was not surprised.

He had a good breakfast, reading first the *Mirror* then P. G. Wodehouse. Pale sun contrived to throw a few shadows on the cloth. The prospect of soon boarding a ship clad in a fortune, and running the gauntlet of U-boats began to give him a Woosterish sense of euphoria. The greasy expanse of calm water stretching it seemed into infinity struck him now as merely being the *friendly* sea, the same that his father's yacht had crossed to take them all to Taormina in 1939. With any luck this Cubitt governess might be a good egg and let him do what he liked on the boat.

After a bit more Wooster he blew back into the old nuptial chamber to find Poppy glued as usual to the blower.

'Look,' he interrupted. 'What's the form?'

She looked up and held up a hand.

'So you'll let us know,' she rapped. 'O.K. . . . O.K. . . . Yupp we'll keep in touch. If you don't get us, leave a message downstairs.' She rang off.

'God!' she said roughly. 'Your sailing's still postponed.'

And Jakey still hadn't rung!

She sagged into her broken-neck position on the pillow to stare out sideways at the white sky and the dirty gable opposite.

Tim sat and swung his pen-knife to and fro on its chain. To and fro, to and fro. Then he fiddled with the blades; then he tried to gouge a screw in the back of one of the chairs.

'What's the drill?' he said.

She looked at him like a dog seeing a ghost. And as though to rub in this doubt Duff looked at him also, like a dog seeing a ghost.

She said: 'Are you all right, darling, for half an hour?'

'Could you make your questions a little more intelligible?'

'I want to get up.'

'Where and when do we rally?'

'Here in half an hour.'

'Right!' he said like a master. 'Break for billiards,' and he looked at his watch. 'I'll be back here at exactly 11.12, my time. Is that understood . . . ? While you annoint yourself yet again from steering-wheel to back axle.'

While she was dressing Jakey rang.

'Darling!' she said fast, fast as '*snap*' and her eyes took on that look of vision which was always most acute when unfocused.

And she told him straight away of the deferred sailing, adding, 'Get this. You're not fixing those toy telescopes till the convoy goes.'

The voice said nothing.

'Are you?' she wanted to know.

'What's Tim up to? What are we going to do?' the voice said.

'I gotta chum,' she said. 'Right here. He used to import Irish ponies for me. He's got a house in the town . . . No, really.'

'What are you hatching, Poppy?'

She protested, described Jimmy. 'You'll love him,' she promised. 'And Tim will love him.'

'Tim will love him . . .'

'What?' she protested. '. . . Sure. Then we can take a little walk.'

'You think of everything.'

'I should be Prime Minister,' she said with a touch of penitence.

'How's Tim taking it?'

'He's O.K. . . . Sure, he's O.K. Why?'

The voice made no comment.

'Yupp. He's pleased. He's pleased as punch with his little coaty-coat,' Poppy laughed coarsely.

'What d'you mean?'

'Just you wait,' she said. 'And how are you?'

Although Poppy made fun, to his face, of her lover's 'murmuring' heart she never *entirely* forgot it and was even aware at fleeting moments of the amount that she moved him around.

His refusal to answer struck her as hypochondriacal.

'How's the ticker?' she said robustly.

He said he had got in at three and that was why he hadn't rung earlier.

'Three!' She was impressed. The ship might have left at midday, and she herself a few hours later. Which would have meant his travelling all that way for half a morning with her.

'I'll give you a little treat,' she promised in a low voice. 'This time.'

His silence suggested that he would believe it when it happened.

'No, I will,' she said.

'When shall I come round,' he said like a *courier*.

She told him.

18

The owner of the daily voice, Jakey de Mornay lay in lemon-silk pyjamas at a temporary 'club' for officers. The ceiling was cracked, the windows grimy and the telephone had been in the passage, as in a hospital. Back on his bed he stared up. Without his highly-powered glasses he looked helpless, like a discharged curate—a soft bodied vertebrate without its shell. And to a certain extent, he *felt* helpless—a sort of human seal. After all, what in God's name, he asked himself, was he doing in the Londonderry Club, Liverpool? Where would he be next? It depended on Poppy. He just lay there admitting: he was her slave. There might have been some hope of a way out, if only he could have wanted one. But he didn't. And he knew he didn't, so he had to admit, being perceptive, that he had taken leave of his senses, as well as of his liberty.

How had it happened?

He was courteous . . . *all over*: his nose was courteous, his very short-sightedness seemed an act of discretion, the softness of his palm was disarming, his pigmentation was unobtrusive, his little pot-belly confiding and generous, like the breast of a milking mother, his dispassion so emulsive that it was difficult to imagine even a Jew-baiting brown shirt in action against Jakey. And he was clever enough to be a little bit unreasonable, thus avoiding the pitfall of exasperating people by being entirely reasonable, which nevertheless (people felt) he might be if he ever wished to try.

Son of a bankrupt Belgian manufacturer and an English

wife he had been through the mill of British upper-class education, owing to the insistence of a rich maiden-aunt who pleasured her last years with a dream of her nephew's future—decreeing it, as far as possible, in her will.

At his preparatory school he had felt as though he had not a single qualification for survival unless it were the 'de' in the middle of his French name. This 'de' had become so important to him that he had engraved it on his locker—for which he had been flogged. Before the beating the master said, 'You're not even French,' an accusation based on school fee cheques from a bank in Brussels.

Then Stowe and Oxford!

By now his very toenails were those of an English gentleman, and as for his gloves, shoes, officer's cane, cigarette case and so on, they all came from the same acre, north of the Ritz, and sometimes put his life's cause in jeopardy simply by being what in Paris or Brussels they could never have been, *too* 'correct.'

Jakey had made money. His deliberating manner (born of horrible dilemmas) had given potential investors a vague sense that here if anywhere lay those coveted still waters which ran securely deep. And for once they had been right. Jakey took shares as they rose from the ground. In vain had he tried to do the same with pheasants, week after week attending shooting schools on the outskirts of London all through the thirties, right up to the declaration of war. But he was still missing on September 3rd, just as in Threadneedle Street, he seldom missed, not even on September 2nd.

People said he was Jewish; even Bertrand, whose maternal grandmother had come from a Mediterranean ghetto, would mutter with malicious finality that Jakey was Jewish as though nothing more need be said. In fact Jakey was descended from Huguenot French and north country Quaker; though his soft, sensitive eyes, stowed away for life behind the thick lens of his glasses, may have been battered in an expression that was 'Jewish.' 'Toasting Jakey' had been the solution, at his prep school, of many a rainy Sunday afternoon. Since then, apart from making money and receiving invitations from certain houses where his advice entitled him to far more than he actually received, nothing serious except his perpetual mother had ever happened to him till he met Poppy. The collision coincided roughly with 'joining up' and felt (to him) like a double liberation, long before that word became common currency. Indeed he was so surprised by both that it took all the change of clothes and a different office to help him believe either. Naturally he had volunteered for service on September 4th and was now battling with former clients, also now in khaki, to have himself upgraded medically so he could risk death. Why? When life was suddenly salty? Perhaps he preferred to be killed by a nation he detested than by a person he adored. Meanwhile: revenge. Jardine-Matherson, who had turned the spit, on which he had been hung for toasting, had borne a marked resemblance particularly in *manner* to Bertrand. Even a saint, in Jakey's position, would have felt that now at last he was toasting Jardine-Matherson . . . scoring goals with his hammer-toes and his French compliments, which Poppy, whose formal education ended at fourteen, answered in misspelt fragments taken from the asides of Charles Boyer. So much for the past. Even so, when gossip first linked the names of Poppy and Jakey, people said: 'I don't believe it!'

In fact what happened was quite straightforward.

She was lying ill, wracked by migraine, curled up on a sofa in a dark and deserted room into which his short-sightedness had carried him in search of the bridge table he had just left. At first he didn't recognise her. She appeared to be the same shape and size as his ebullient hostess, but there all similarity stopped like a road coming to a blown bridge.

'Poppy . . . ?' he said furtively . . . 'Poppy . . . ?' and then, horrified by his intrusion on tears, 'I'm so sorry!' and averting his eyes he moved to the door. Then something made him pause, perhaps a memory of another tear-stained face, swinging from three billiard cues, trussed into one, another loud voice, savagely peremptory, saying 'Now poke the coals' as Bertrand had just shouted at her '*You led diamonds!*'

Yes, he paused but he still didn't really believe that that *sight* could really be Poppy. Only a few hours earlier he had called her a bully (respectfully of course) to her face and she had said, 'That's right, soon I'll pull back those little hammer-toes of yours and we'll see if you can get a pheasant that way,' making everyone laugh—at his embarrassment and at the disrespectful knowledge of his intimate parts which she was pleased to flaunt.

So he could only marvel. He had often seen Bertrand sitting in the middle of swathes of blue smoke in claret-coloured velvet, eating his moustache, uneasy, shouting and fidgeting in and out of his monogrammed slippers like a caricature from *Krokodil* and believed him to have been at last subjugated (as people continually alleged) by his wise-cracking child-bride who rode horses high as a house and flirted with bishops.

Could this here be the alleged victor?

'May I offer you a larger handkerchief?' he had dared to say.

A sheet would have been more appropriate. He had wondered where so much liquid came from: she seemed to be dissolving.

'Dear Poppy,' he had murmured. And then, 'On these occasions an outsider is really more than ever an outsider. But I'd like you to know that at this moment I honour and respect you much more than ever before. I think you're sweet.'

His spectacles had steamed over.

'Stay,' she had said.

Oh! like a child!

'Stay with me!' she had said.

Music was one of his things, but he had never heard any till then.

And he stayed.

19

Tim returned to his stepmother's room and was not surprised to hear she had a friend in Liverpool. She had had one in Gibraltar. Besides the name Jakey was vaguely familiar. One of the Zombies, he thought. One more unfortunate jester who did not even have the privilege of making the jests. There was that picture dealer in Newcastle who came over to Garston and squealed with delight whenever she put him on a dangerous horse or insulted him. Presumably, this Jakey chap was a picture dealer of Liverpool who filled the bill equally well.

'You've met him,' Poppy said. She was finishing off her face.

'But while you two roar your heads off with youthful laughter, what happens to me?'

'We're all going to Jimmy's.' She got up, nestling into her broad leather belt, like a girth but studded with brass. The smell of her scent must have made flies faint.

He began swinging his knife again.

'Jimmy Lennox,' she said. 'A trainer. He got me Grasshopper.'

'*Horses*,' he complained. 'I might have guessed.' They came second after women on his black list. And he remembered now: he had seen Jakey hunting at Garston, a small man who had given him two pounds instead of one, on departure, and asked to see his dinosaur bones. A thin black lace had attached his top-hat to his riding coat.

Tim felt vaguely encouraged.

Poppy talked, and made him put on his 'life-jacket.' He protested but she was adamant. Then they went down and sat in the lounge, in front of the big window, he in the purplish coat.

'Stop feeling it. It looks O.K. What are you complaining about?'

'Possibly,' he said, 'he'll consent to show up before we turn into stalactites, listening to each other's drip.'

A page boy soon came to the door and gestured in their direction, then Jakey appeared in cavalry breeches and service dress, like a picture from the previous war. Not really so very different from the meet at Garston, when Tim had first seen him. Poppy went to him and allowed herself to be fondled like a cat, turning in and around against him, while he enfolded her with one arm and held out the other, 'And Tim,' he said kindly as though here was another, almost equal pleasure. 'Dear Tim!'

Tim was inches taller than both of them. Having taken the moist hand he said, 'What's the programme?'

Somehow Jakey had acquired a car. But didn't wish the matter referred to.

'A business friend,' he said and his thin mouth smiled as though aware what horrors that phrase might not cover. Then:

'Tim dear, has Poppy asked you *once* what you want to do on your last day? Or has she made up your mind for you?'

'You've said it,' Tim said.

She bridled, appealed mockingly with her big brown eyes for Tim's good opinion. 'I've been a liddle sister to him—tucked him up, everything!'

Tim groaned and Jakey looked from one to the other,

gently, with big big spectacles, which had given so many clients the feeling that here at last was the crystal ball they needed—two crystal balls, side by side, like range-finders.

'You didn't bring Caroline and Georgina?' Jakey inquired. 'My pin-ups! How are they?'

Tim was embarrassed by the suggestion that he should feel fond of his stepsisters and annoyed by Jakey's ignorance of recent events.

'They are somewhat outside my province,' he replied. 'Possibly you had better consult their mother.'

'They're patriots,' Poppy said, 'sticking it out, with Mother.' This portrait of herself as Boadicea caused Jakey to smile.

But Tim said: 'Cur-reist! That'll be the day.'

'What will be the day?' Poppy said.

'When they even see you.'

'He's jealous,' she said. 'We'd better move.'

'Then shall we go, Poppy dear? . . . Tim, shall we go?' and Jakey held out both hands like wings.

On the stairs Jakey said: 'Where's she taking us?'

Tim shrugged.

Poppy called back, 'Forty-two Light Street.'

Jakey smiled at Tim as much as to say, *Let's take a ride on the Giant Poppy*.

But Tim suspected that Jakey *knew something*. He had strung along too easily, even for a Zombie.

'I suppose you know this Mr. Lennox?' Tim said.

'I've heard of him once,' said Jakey. 'Half an hour ago.'

'Then what's the object of the operation?'

'A liddle fun,' Poppy said.

'FUN,' Tim yelled hitting the wall with the back of his fist. 'That's rich!'

'D'you like his coat?' Poppy said, turning.

'It's a nice coat,' Jakey said.

'You lecture *me* . . .' Tim cried.

'All right, all right!' she interrupted, gagging him and laughed.

'What's happening?' Jakey said.

She had them both: one on one hook, one on the other: two males, in tandem. Two-in-hand. Flirting and driving.

'Slit her gullet,' Tim said.

'Now just be good,' she said. 'Just follow Aunt Poppy.'

'Famous last words,' Tim said.

But Jakey smiled and was happy: he was giving her liberty and looking after Bertrand's son. And he was with her.

They drove for miles. They got lost. They argued. Tim stared up at walls, hoardings, chimneys, warehouses and the faces of passers-by describing through the window their ignorance of Light Street.

'*When* you've finished,' he said.

But at last Jakey was able to say, 'There! . . . There's Light Street for you,' peering up as he spoke at a smoky legend on the corner of a long row of houses such as Tim had only seen in articles about miners and unemployed.

'Jesus Christ,' he said. 'Are you *quite* mad?'

Her laughter thrived on their faces.

Jakey permitted himself a thin smile.

'We're just interested,' he said as he carefully drove down one side, noting the faded numbers on the peeling walls. There was a bomb gap, recent enough to be still a shambles; flanked by mean wall-paper leprous with damp.

'I saw an aspidistra,' Jakey said. 'It shows they're inhabited.'

Many windows were blown out, and two walls were propped by flying buttresses of rough carpentry, heavy beams and big black bolts and screws.

'We're coming to the sea if you really want to know,' Tim said, seeing a funnel.

Poppy laughed as though suddenly drunk.

'Hotel Madras!' Jakey said. 'Forty-one.'

Then there it was: Forty-two.

'Carry on, driver,' Tim said.

'I think so too,' Jakey said quietly.

'God, you're snobs,' Poppy said, got out and went to the door. No bell. But the knocker worked. And she worked it, looking back at them, downwards as though from a stage, scorning them.

Tim and Jakey followed. Tim mutinous, Jakey protective.

The woman who opened the door closed it again a little on sight. Her disappointed eyes said 'police.' She raised a damp rag to her nose and mouth and waited to hear the worst.

Miss Margaret Lennox.

She had often been called on, in the past, by people who were not welcome. Strangers, in particular, had proved always to fall into this category and certainly the three whom she now saw were strangers. None stranger! She hardly opened the door at all. She had hoped it was Mrs. Oliphant.

'Well,' she said in a low voice. Every syllable might be used against her though Father Doyle would speak for her as one who had never gone wrong, no matter what about her brother or sister or niece.

Jakey saluted her. He would have saluted any female. But Miss Lennox, his manner suggested, made the ceremony a pleasure.

'Does Mr. Jimmy Lennox live here?' Poppy said.

Miss Lennox was not surprised. After a moment's hesitation, she invited them in, leading them back into a dingy room that smelt of old boiled cabbage and coal dust.

A fire burned in the range with a flame no bigger than that of a candle, but a kettle was singing placidly as though all were really better than it seemed. Some dirty clothes lay on the linoleum table-cover but these Miss Lennox put out of sight as she leaned this way and that, preparing chairs, within reach of each other. On the mantelpiece were a few ornaments such as Tim had nearly won, yesterday, at the Edgware Road amusement park, and two small candlesticks, a long fringed cloth along the mantelpiece that was vaguely reminiscent of an altar if not a catafalque. Here, it seemed, in this cramped space, a difficult aspiration had been stated.

'Will you sit down,' Miss Lennox said, 'and I'll see if I can't fetch Jimmy. Who shall I say it is?'

She said this like a medium.

But Poppy thought she spoke well; she must have been in service; perhaps a cook.

'Lady Bewick,' Poppy said. 'Say Springfields—1938. He got a pony for me from James O'Reilly . . . Grasshopper.' Her voice had taken on its pressing tone as though refusing in advance to be contradicted—least of all by Jakey whom she now turned to and stared out.

Miss Lennox went.

Then Poppy looked at Tim.

'What's the matter with you?' she said.

'What's the matter with YOU, you mean,' Tim said angrily.

Jakey said, 'What a pretty budgie!'

Poppy looked at the bird and its tiny cage in which it made continuously the miraculous but unmistakable noise of joy—a kind of fidgety hopeful whispering that went well with its exquisite markings and colour like the palest blue of some infinite, sunny midday.

'Yupp,' Poppy said. 'A priddy bird . . . in some cage!'

Miss Lennox had not far to go to find her brother. Upstairs he was lying twenty feet away in the room which he had been sharing, to her shame and misery, with his niece. *Her* niece also, Maureen, who at the sound of visitors had already disappeared at the back. Mrs. Oliphant from the Missions had already once got her re-evacuated.

'Jim . . . ?' Miss Lennox said.

Unlike his sister Jimmy lived in perpetual hope of visitors: there was a man coming one day who would give him his due. But this morning the flesh was weak. He could only say 'Wassat?' with but a small part of the hope which still existed in him somewhere.

She explained—without respect for his condition.

'Ther'y'are,' he said reverently. 'Lady Bewick! What did I say?'

'Have you got clothes fit to be seen . . . ?'

She went back to announce that he was coming, not mentioning that he would first have to dress.

She offered tea and biscuits. Jakey accepted as though relieved of intolerable thirst and hunger. Poppy asked about bombs: she'd seen damage, she said.

Miss Lennox bore no grudge against unknown people, provided they weren't nosey. She thought Jakey a pleasant gentleman, like a Mr. Wilson, whom she used to work for. And after a few looks in his direction she even began to feel about him as she felt about Father Doyle, except Father Doyle never had time to stay long. It wasn't often she got the opportunity to talk to anyone who would listen without contradicting and since her niece was back and the shame that kept her at home, hardly ever. But at first she answered little—a few monosyllables. Then Jakey said:

'I saw a rather pretty little church as we came along and the date 1670. I was surprised.'

Miss Lennox stood at the edge of the table and considered him further; yes, a neat little officer-gentleman with a soft face, not unlike that of the late Father Birrel, he was, and asking about the past: she felt the years well up inside her like a great storm. A desire to weep touched her. She raised her handkerchief and tidied the end of her nose.

'Yes,' she said coolly. 'And there's older than that!'

Jakey said, 'Have you always lived here . . . ?'

Her eyes misted over. It was too much for her.

Her mother, in this room, bathing them on Saturdays from three kettles. And now Maureen! Up to anything! Not her fault. She began then. Looking earnestly at her questioner. 'We were fourteen children. My father died just after the youngest was born. That was in 1914. My oldest brother was the only one old enough to work like and went to a printers where he had seven shillings a week . . . then the war came and he couldn't get away quick enough. He told his age wrong and got taken. He went to Gallipoli and was invalided out after trouble with his eyes. I remember him coming home, straight to the pier down there. Then he got married, but soon took his mother's name so as to be taken back into the army. And he got back. As a medical orderly. To France. He did so well they said he could have become a doctor if he'd had the education. He stayed a sergeant after the armistice but developed this whatsit sclerosis; they said he'd started it in the trenches with his eyes, see. They had a hard time. He couldn't get his pension because he'd changed his name like to get back into the army, see: he wasn't eligible. He used to say he didn't exist like, so his sclerosis didn't exist.'

Poppy's expression changed from whimsicality to morose absorption in the biography which Jakey had unleashed.

The old voice went on, quavering a bit: 'He got very bitter and wrote a pamphlet which a friend of his was going to publish but nothing came of it, I don't think. Then Colonel Scott the M.P. got up a subscription. It was in the papers he had a wheeled chair from it. Afterwards the Prince of Wales sent him three pounds. So the papers came again and took a picture of him with the envelope and the crest. That's how the

National Assistance people heard of it. They made him pay back the three pounds by five shilling instalments. It was that or give up the Assistance. No one believed it even then. But it was all true. And he soon died.'

Poppy had played golf with the Prince of Wales. She sat, very upright, on the edge of her chair, knees slanting, slack, to one side, looking at Miss Lennox with complete acceptance, as though she, Poppy, *had become* Miss Lennox, a phenomenon which was naturally marked by feelings of despair, as clearly visible in her expression as giants in the eyes of a five-year-old told a story at bed-time. Perhaps that was why Miss Lennox went on, looking now more and more at Poppy.

'We thought it was worse for him because we'd never been really poor. The poor were more over that side—Scotland Road way. 'Course my mother had a job: we never got no medicine except Togo we called it, slices of turnip with brown sugar. She'd put turnip in a jam jar and sugar and then turnip and so on, bottled for a week: if one got it one day, he went without the next and so on. You never got it twice running except you were very bad. She could have got clothes for us, "police clothes" they were called, from the Cathedral, corduroys and clogs but the corduroy smelt awful and everyone knew it like, a sort of uniform. No matter how bad things were, people would do anything to go without "police clothes." We managed somehow and never took police clothes.'

Poppy made a sound of deep approval.

'But things have changed. Mother wouldn't believe it . . .' She seemed about to weep and then collected herself: 'The Mission was good and Miss Williams at the school gave her life for us children down there and we all did well except the ones that died. We had two with T.B. and now I've the youngest brother with it here now. He's next door. I've a sister who's a nurse in London and another in the Fuel office; and a brother who's a joiner in Canada. This is the house where we were all born. Now there's only Jimmy and my brother Tom.'

Poppy moved her eyes, turned her head away.

'I'm looking after Tom when I'm not on night shift in the factory. He's got T.B. in the next room. He hasn't got much longer. Margaret Mcilroy from next door comes in and sits with him. She's dying of cancer but she says she won't mind if she dies in here. So when the bombs fall she gets under his bed. She says it's where she wants to be, underneath him, when she dies . . . And Jimmy talks to him now and again, and cheers him up: Jimmy was to be an actor . . .'

A wan smile again loosened Miss Lennox's susceptible mouth. The memory of her brother long ago was no help to the reality of him now. 'He always went his own way . . .' she said, hearing him move in the passage. 'But now he's back . . ' and she looked sideways as though the opportunity for speech was now at an end, certainly for her, probably for everyone else too. And she took no responsibility for anything to do with him.

Poppy was bewildered. There could be no doubt about Grasshopper. He had even been quite a good pony. Surely she had not made a mistake . . .

She looked expectantly at the passage, like Jakey and Tim. But nothing emerged.

'He's . . . slow,' Miss Lennox said.

'What happened to his business?' Poppy said.

Miss Lennox looked a bit visionary for a moment and then put the lid over a piece of margarine.

'You mean when he was with Joe Powers for a bit, the bookie?'

'Springfields,' Poppy said.

Miss Lennox moved her head very slightly as though objecting.

'Yes, there was a Springfields . . .' she said.

Poppy's eyebrows raised high and she turned to Jakey for support. In what? She turned farther—to Tim, smiling at him as though here, even here, was a joke. He gave her a withering look and turned away looking out into the damp grey misty street.

Soon he would be floating out where it might be even greyer, certainly damper, stranger.

The noise in the passage reached a crescendo of wheezing and shuffling.

'Here he is then!' Miss Lennox said. 'I'll be getting along,' and she squeezed past the fat figure who appeared unshaved with red-rimmed eyes in a black suit and huge red handkerchief hanging from his breast pocket like the gory entrail of some royal beast whom the cruel hunters had caught at last. He raised both hands towards them all:

'God alive,' he murmured reverently. 'It's Poppy!'

Then Poppy took up life again: because at heart she asked always only this: to be crowned. She rose. Submitted to an embrace, laughing. Tim was frightened; Jakey concerned: there were limits, hygienic ones.

'And what's happened to yooo!' Poppy drawled at her old friend of two years—or was it two minutes?—ago.

'Bombed right out of me hotel. And look at this!' sighting Tim.

'Her own brother,' he marvelled, 'beautiful as the lights of Bootle on a summer night . . . No, don't laugh!' he said severely. 'God, look at that then! Right here in my own place, the son of Connachar, in the April of life, with eyes full of dreams still unspecified. Where's Maureen . . . . ?

'Maureen,' he called, towards the passage.

The cobwebs were clearing from his mind and opportunity taking shape.

In producing his niece he expected to give a fillip to that idea of himself which must have persisted in Poppy's memory to bring her here; any idea of 'breeding' racehorses and beauty. But he had to call again: 'Let's have a sight of you then' (he could hear her at the back). 'She has her uncle's modesty . . .'

In time a girl appeared at the door. She was dark in a thin grey dress, ill-fitting with a torn pocket and a gaudy belt; her make-up was conspicuous, each colour separate from the other, like paint on a bad picture. Here was childhood in travesty—only her eyes seemed to have seen as much as Poppy's but come to a different conclusion, and perhaps her body too. But it was particularly her eyes that claimed attention—large, and surprisingly soft.

Everyone, even Tim, stared.

On her neck was the smudge of a large mole. Her hair touched her shoulders, falling from two 'horns' and as she appeared she gave it a jerk sideways, a gesture she reinforced by opening her jaws and shifting a wad of gum from the front of her mouth to the back where she tucked it in flat with a slow downward movement of her molars. The nipples of her young breasts were clearly visible through the thin material of her dress.

'There!' Jimmy said rather in the manner of a conjurer who is not sure what he had produced from the hat, 'Maureen!'

Jakey held out a hand. Maureen wiped hers on her dress which was already dappled with stains and took his. At the same instant, she dropped a vestigial curtsy.

'The nuns that took her away,' Jimmy explained.

Maureen accepted the explanation without any reaction.

Poppy was ill at ease with all women, able to feel them as nothing but competitors, unless they were in her pay or as old as mothers, preferably both. Dirt too, however relished or laughed at in kennels or hospital adventures, became an allergy when encountered unofficially and in private. She did not put out her hand; but took in Maureen's face and figure swiftly, almost furtively, and then turned away raising her eyebrows very high and dropping her eyes while her mouth flickered gauchely—a mannerism which often was the preliminary, Jakey knew, to some of her worst, most outrageous remarks. But the moment passed, safely.

Tim had risen to his feet.

'Hi,' he said.

Maureen again shifted the gum from one side of her mouth to the other revealing in the process, saliva, teeth, tongue and for a moment a grey bundle of compressed Spearmint. Then she rested her back against the wall and took in the guests with the confidence of one who didn't usually have to wait long to find the explanation of even the most surprising phenomena . . . Except Tim. There, on him, her eyes stayed.

Silence fell.

Poppy looked at Jakey.

Jimmy knew he had to grasp something quickly.

He said, 'Listen to this': he did something with his arms to fill the space of words, till they came. Like a conductor marking a break . . .

'She's just back to-day. " Look," I said to the lady in the city chambers, "her mother's dead, her father's been torpedoed three times and caught such a cold he's warming himself with spirit for the rest of time, in ten years she had only one sure thing—myself," ' he pointed to himself. ' "But what do you do," I said, "for God's sake: You evacuate her to Chester to save her from the Jerrybombs. You billet her next the station and the very first night she's blown right out of bed. God alive," I said, "and what do you do with her by day? Education? Not at arl. She was run over twice the first week. And what about her morals? The sweepings of all the gaols in Canada have come to the help of the King in England but nobody thought of a thing to do with them. Various young criminals with a single wish. So what do we do in Welfare?

Evacuate our maidens within reach of them!" No . . . no, listen . . . I've sat over there, right there,' and he pointed at the wooden chair, '. . . in my hotel that was bombed and *wept*!' He paused with fearful effect, relishing their faces. The pause was perfectly timed: he broke it with a fierce thump on his chest and: ' "*Give her back*," I said. "Give her back this instant. If she's to be blown up, raped and altogether made miserable then let all of these things come to pass where she has just the one sure thing she's ever known: Jimmy Lennox." '

A tear leaked from his convinced eyes.

Tim was distracted at last. Suddenly Jimmy's hand shot out sideways with the index finger pointing straight at his face.

'Would you send your brother away out of sight for ever into jeopardy just for fear of a Jerrybomb . . . *would you*? Well, then! That's all I mean. We're all flesh and blood. Now Poppy and you, sir, you drive in a fine car and live in a great house, Poppy, for the difference is largely illusion. So you'll see what I mean when I tell you I said this: "*Give her back by Tuesday!*" '

'So they did,' Poppy said limply.

Jimmy hesitated. 'Nothing of the kind . . . she came back on her own.'

He waved contemptuously at the door.

'That's why she wasn't here to welcome you. She thought you were a Nun, Poppy, or Mrs. Olly-fant . . .'

Maureen smiled.

A dull intuitive gleam lit his eyes. The idea of such a mistake amused them both. Poppy turned from them.

'Well?' she said to Jakey. 'Prraps . . . ? We had better . . . ?'

Tim stirred hopefully.

20

He wanted to go. For half an hour now he had tried to avoid seeing, or smelling and when Miss Lennox started on her life story, even listening. He moved a step towards the door, in the firm belief that his stepmother's latest stunt was over.

'You're on yar leave from the Army?' said Jimmy.

Tim flushed and said aggressively, 'I'm on my way to America, thank heavens.'

Jimmy was theatrically shocked—and turned to Poppy.

'I shan't believe it,' he whispered.

'Yupp,' she said. 'He's getting out.'

Tim looked at her.

Jimmy said, 'You'd leave your father to fetch the coal by himself . . .' and he touched Tim who recoiled slightly.

Poppy laughed. Jimmy went on, now holding Tim in his strong hands and staring into the side of his averted face as though he were a skin specialist, declaring Tim's desire to go to America was not what it seemed.

Tim leaned away from Jimmy's breath but there was no avoiding it.

'Would you *kindly* take your paws off?' he suddenly burst out.

Jimmy froze. At last he whispered.

'He's going to knock me down! . . . Take off your coat then, Timmy boy!'

'NO,' guffawed Poppy. 'That's the last thing he must do!' and she turned to Jakey doubled over with laughter.

Jimmy said, 'Wassat? . . . He'll catch cold, will he?' Jimmy looked at her with his speckly eyes gone dreamy in the effort to pick up the right thread from a maze of possibilities.

'It's just that he's had a cold,' Poppy said.

'A cold! Then he'd be better in the warm. Do you play billiards?'

'There you are,' Poppy said triumphantly.

'Maureen,' Jimmy said. 'Show your guest the billiards where it's warm in the Hotel Madras.'

'Go on—little man,' Poppy teased. 'What did I tell you?'

'What did you tell him?' Jimmy said.

'Oh, for Christ's sake,' Tim said.

'That he'd have a lovely time at Jimmy's,' Poppy said.

'He's scared,' Jimmy said.

Tim went. Wouldn't anyone?

'I'd like to get us all a nice stiff drink,' Jakey said. 'But where?'

He rose and took from his pocket a slim pig-skin wallet in which the pound notes and fivers lay together as though ironed.

'Put all that away!' Jimmy whispered ominously. 'Where does he come from?' he asked Poppy sadly. Then he yelled 'MAUREEN!'

She came back and looked at him.

'Ask Mrs. Leroy for a bottle on your way.'

She hesitated but he made a sign. When she had gone they all looked lost.

Jimmy thirrupped his fingers on the table and sighed when he caught Poppy's eyes on the furniture.

No interior imaginable could have stood in sharper contrast to her memories of Jimmy in 1938.

He heaved another heavier sigh. 'Isn't it a turrible war,' he said.

'What happened to the horses at Springfields?' Poppy said.

He brightened.

'There was no sense in it: they said certain ones were to be kept in stock but the man that came round didn't know a pig from a cow. It was who you knew that decided their fate. So I hadn't a chance. They took the lot off me for sausages. My living went. Pht! God, I was crying when they walked them away to the vans. Stardust, Androcles, Twice Two, Tobermory, Answer Me Now. Atta Boy . . . "Don't you want the blankets?" they said.' He threw out his hands for mercy. ' "What," I said. Even the revolutionaries in France didn't send the kings and queens to the knife naked. "But they're good blankets," they said . . .' He held up his hand as though bidding peace for ever to such voices. ' "Put them on your beds," I said, "they might inform you in dreams what you've done!" '

'Don't,' Poppy said. 'It was ghastly. They knew. You could see it in their eyes.' She looked sickened.

Jakey's eyes fell and he touched his spectacles. His relationship with field sports in the twentieth century had been part of a complicated and painful exercise in personal camouflage. To be expected to share the emotions either of the quarry or the saddled conveyance had never occurred to him. But this *séance* was typical of Poppy and he smiled weakly, as though discovering, too late, that he was having an affair with a flying mare.

'They knew—you could see it!' Poppy cried. 'Venus had diarrhoea after the first lot went. From then on—she was waiting for the footsteps at first light . . .' Her eyes hardened.

Jimmy groaned: 'It's the principle that's dangerous. You put down your horse on Monday; be God it's your mother on Thursday!'

She was puzzled. She had no mother to put down; besides the order of fatality should have been reversed to be touching. She said: 'Wuell . . . where will it end?' burlesquing the bromide in a strange drawl so as to save her insincerity from complete nakedness. She lived so intensely in the present that where 'things' ended was always the most futile abstraction. If she'd lived anyhow else she wouldn't be here.

'I hid six in a quarry,' she said. 'Now they pull milk under false names.' She turned to Jakey. 'You sit there like a stuffed owl but I saw Emir in Gateshead, only last week. They've got him on coal. Nosebag. Medallions, the lot. I had a word with the driver. He knew at once. Said he tied false hair round his hocks on the first Tuesday of the month. That's when the boffins come round.'

Jimmy marvelled at her. And she at him. They believed each other. No wonder they had come together again. 'And d'you ever get out riding any more?' he said reverently.

'I took the Home Secretary. He'd never been on a horse.'

'The Home Secretary!'

'Yupp. He was visiting. Gaols. I went with him. He loves me.'

'God!' . . . Jimmy encouraged. 'Go on.' He was moving high.

'First cell we went into he said, "Why are you here?" "Conscientious Objector, sir." So I said to the Conchy, "Cheer up: you'll be Home Secretary in the next war!" '

'You said that!—And why?'

'Because that's what the Home Secretary *was* in the first war—a Conchy!'

'Listen to that! What did he say?'

'He wasn't pleased, till he got outside. Then he laughed. He loves me.' Poppy looked at Jakey but he wouldn't meet her eyes. But the other man couldn't look at anything else.

'I love you too,' he said quietly.

Jakey didn't.

'*Well,*' she protested to Jakey. 'He WAS a conscientious objector in the First War. I'm not condemning him. Perhaps he's just a nice little guy with a squint.' She made herself laugh.

Jakey quoted, ' "If you must talk . . ." '

Poppy finished for him, ' "talk victory." Meanwhile pass the pea-shooter and rally the Home Guard with a banana-skin to put under the German tanks. Perhaps when the Yankee-doodles have made enough money out of us, they'll step in to save a good customer. If we hadn't had ten years of Mr. Chamberpot and the Boneless Wonder we might be doing a bit better!'

'Listen to that!' Jimmy said.

'Or rather, don't,' Jakey advised.

'WELL . . . ?' Poppy exploded. 'What d'you expect. You all sit around in Sam Brownes saying Hip-hip-hooray to whatever anyone says or does. What are you doing? Now you're touring the country fitting discarded spectacles on to A.A. guns . . . Hamley's Toobs!'

'Poppy!' Jakey commanded.

Jimmy was fascinated. He wanted her to go on but Maureen appeared with the whisky, looking strangely at her uncle. He did not meet her eyes but took the bottle. Jakey put money on the window-sill.

'Where have you put Junior?' Poppy asked.

Maureen stared at the apparition with wide, expressionless eyes so that Poppy made a slight face and turned away smiling as much as to say: Well, what have I said now: can't she answer?

'There's a kind of annexe,' Jimmy said, 'you might say adjacent where I have some interest. A place for billiards and the odd game of chance where some of our old friends will foregather of an evening and talk of the great days behind.'

'D'you mean he's gambling?'

'He's at hand,' Jimmy said, 'just a few minutes away. The thing about the place is the warmth of it and the billiards.'

Silence fell and Jakey looked expectantly at Poppy.

She said, 'Wurrl . . . we're disturbing you. We ought to get on.'

'But you'll take a drink?'

'When we come back.' She got up, seeing him holding hands with the bottle like a fiancée, limp with desire.

'What about Tim?' Jakey said.

'Tim adores billiards. Could he stay with you and Maureen? We've got some shopping to do. Just till lunch.'

'Why not all day?' Jimmy said.

'O. Kayee—if your sister can keep an eye on them.'

Jakey said, 'We'll see him as we go.'

The ground floor of the Madras was a sleazy café with a big tea urn and 'No cigarettes' and 'Eggs' pasted on to one side of the steamed-up window. Two workmen were drinking from heavy china cups at little tables; a pale man with a thin, expressionless face nodded to them as they passed from behind the counter.

Upstairs at the back Tim was alone, playing a shot on one of four miniature billiard tables.

'Happy?' Poppy said.

'When are we going back to the hotel?'

Poppy said, 'They're expecting you to lunch.'

The phrase 'expecting you to lunch' with its overtones of life at Garston made him look at her blankly.

'If you honestly think I'm having lunch in that dump you're mistaken!'

Poppy's face locked. 'Just don't *talk* like that,' she said in a low rough voice. 'You're jolly lucky to get any lunch at all.'

Tim closed his eyes and roughed the front of his hair, scratching his head as though it were an alternative to assault. 'Look: *do* you mind . . . I mean *shall* we start again . . . are you *more* bonkers than is generally assumed . . .' he petered out overwhelmed by incoherence and fury.

Poppy then delivered a total judgment: 'The trouble with you is simple: you're spoilt!'

Jakey opened his mouth like a goldfish. No sound came forth.

Tim said, 'Take her away quickly will you.'

Jakey said, 'Tim . . .'

'Take her AWAY!'

'Do you want to come with us?'

'Now *is* that likely?' He walked after the ball which he had struck. Jakey and Poppy remained in silence by the edge of the table. Jakey was torn. And concerned. He saw how it must be for Tim. All the same he could not bring himself to blame Poppy, not even when her voice took on the hectoring tones of a Victorian governess. He interceded, putting the matter to Tim squarely and finally as between adults: would he prefer to come back or stay here?

Tim said he would sooner stay anywhere else in the world than with them.

'Don't *talk* like that,' Poppy said.

It was she who was lingering now.

'Then you'll stay here with Jimmy?' Jakey said.

Tim bent to another shot.

Jakey said, 'If you like, Tim—we could all go to a cinema.'

Poppy said, 'He's seen everything that's on. He told me. Here he's got some roly-poly balls and a liddle playmate.' She was nagging him, in revenge for his contempt.

Tim said, 'Good-bye,' and hit the ball so hard it raced several times round the table.

They moved towards the door.

'D'you want to take my coat with you by any chance?'

Poppy stopped dead. 'Golly!' she said.

'Why should we want your coat?' Jakey said.

'It's his best coat,' Poppy said looking dreamy. Jakey took her arm. At his touch she felt dopey.

She said: 'You'll be all right in it if you don't take it off.'

'O.K. . . .' he said. 'Enjoy yourselves.'

'We'll be back here about three.'

'You needn't hurry.'

They went. 'He's *so* rude,' she complained to Jakey. 'And usually with me he's O.K.'

Jakey was unable to explain the phenomenon.

'If I hadn't brought him, who would?' she protested.

Maureen was on the stairs.

'D'you play billiards?' Poppy asked her.

Maureen wondered at her face as though trying to read the answer in the curious features. 'Snooker,' she said, the word falling like a leaf—after cymbals and brass.

'Teach him snooker,' Poppy said.

Jakey got out his wallet and went back into the room. 'You'll probably go to a little place down the road. Have the best lunch you can get, Tim . . .' and he held out a five-pound note. 'Plenty of ginger pop . . .'

Tim, who had moved away after a ball, said, 'Put it in one of the base pockets please.'

'And if there's anything over buy your host a present.'

Tim had become more and more restless, hitting balls wildly.

'My host,' he said.

'Come along,' Poppy called.

'Here,' Jakey said and popped the fiver into one of the base pockets, as though into a velvet bag at church.

They left, followed by Maureen.

'I thought you were staying?' Poppy said.

'I've to see me uncle,' she said strangely.

They all went.

Tim struck the ball hard.

For a few moments he played shots then he went to the window.

Two figures: Poppy and Jakey crossing the street. Then Maureen who turned down the pavement. As though feeling themselves for the first time safe, Poppy and Jakey came together like two bits of wood floating in water, closing the last inch quickly. In the same way their inner arms came up and out, each drawing the body of the other closer still. Poppy leaned her head a little sideways and even their footsteps fell into a sort of rhythm, like a dance, making them suddenly a quadruped. Then Jakey's arm straightened, pushing her gently away as a soldier appeared saluting him. He responded punctiliously. A moment later Poppy was back, insisting, laughing, till they got to the car. When they got in Tim expected it to move, but it didn't.

The street was empty and dim. Fog made it almost night. Tim turned to the scattered balls. It didn't seem to matter which one he hit—or missed. He had seen a bill for an Edward G. Robinson film which he'd already seen twice. Where was the hotel? 'Only ten minutes.' They'd come in a circle. He thought of his father, of Poppy's figure walking naked towards her bed . . . of Jakey.

She came up here to meet him, he thought. If he couldn't have come, she wouldn't have either. But he managed to make it. Oh, yes, he managed that, and she managed it. Something nameless associated with the idea of them; he hit the balls harder and more viciously, thinking of the coat round his shoulders. Which was why he was here.

On the wall-hooks someone had left a coat-hanger, with a number burnt on the middle.

21

Maureen went quietly into the house but her aunt, who was always listening for her, came out of the back room.

'Where's the boy, Maureen?' she said.

Maureen went up a few steps before answering: 'Playin' billiards.'

'You took him there!'

'What's wrong with there?'

'You should know.'

'Some people's nasty minds.'

'I can get you taken back, Maureen!'

'Shan't be in when they come.'

'Your grandmother and then your mother: fifty years without trouble. Then you, Maureen. Without half the excuse!'

Miss Lennox succeeded in putting into her voice the moral *siege* which this house had withstood over the years. Maureen had to turn from that seared, upturned face, the pointing work-worn hand. Her aunt, she told herself, was stuck, talking of Mother. She always had been. Her very kindness oppressed Maureen with a sense of intolerable obligation. It was no surprise that her Uncle Jimmy always whispered when she was in earshot. Maureen muttered something neutral and went on so that her aunt lost sight of her.

'Don't forget, Maureen! . . . I'm not taking much more!'

The door above slammed—like an answer; and Miss Lennox turned back to the face she had been sponging. 'If her mother knew,' she whispered. She had been telling Tom about the visitors who had come, but now the thread had been broken. *What are they saying up there*, she thought. Better if this one here had lived and worked and that drunk one had played here with old *Daily Mail* puzzles and died.

Miss Lennox frowned, squeezing tepid water from the sponge, hearing her mother say: 'Very well, then. You'll stay in all week after school.' This after seeing any one of her children just *talking* to one of the 'bad' children, the climbers of railings.

Now this, under her own roof! Mother's roof! Maureen!

A nice girl. Only last year a nice girl.

She squeezed the sponge and let it absorb fresh water. To-night she'd have Maureen down sleeping with her, even if it meant another row. She'd win.

Miss Lennox turned to the face, like damp white cheese, of her brother and talked to him of other things.

The room Maureen shared with her uncle had an old screen in the middle and a clothes line slung from window to wall across the front of the fire. Hardly a square inch was unoccupied. On Jimmy's side a vignetted photograph of a stern-looking woman in a black shawl, his mother, looked out as though offended, through a ring of cigarette-cards of racehorses stuck neatly between frame and glass. There were three or four old almanacs, newspapers weighted down by a bible, a chest of drawers, and a mass of utensils and odds and ends. On her side there were pictures of film stars, dirty garments, sweet papers, comics and a coat with grey fur trimmings which she had bought recently. The fur on it always looked wet. And on her pillow a *Romance Weekly*: 'Neath Tropic Skies.' The whole front of this week was a head and shoulders of Conrad, the dark hero.

'He's in the billiards,' she said.

Jimmy was sitting on the bed with the bottle of whisky half empty, on his lap. The pangs of opportunity got through to him. Slowly. His face contracted like that of a child pretending to be asleep. He spoke but it turned into a wheeze. A tremendous sense of achievement and justification lingered in his mind. It prevented him from rising to the occasion—which cried aloud for the sure hand of experience—as he could see by the bewildered face he had never seen bewildered before. A fiver, she now said, was in the billiard table pocket and the boy there alone with a cue . . . He could size it all up, from the smithereens of a vanished past, but how to assemble enough for Maureen to recognise—when his tongue was numb and clumsy as the day the dentist took all his teeth. Communication was easier with a hand. He raised the free one in a gesture that tried to sketch complete absolution for any intention that might have crossed her mind in the interests of their common weal. But even this was too much of a demand on his powers. The hand fell and he groaned at the distance which had thrust itself between him and her.

She waited, touching the crucifix at her neck, vaguely conscious of authority seeping away from her now that she had deferred to him for advice; and in that state! But what could she do, the lady and the boy weren't ordinary, nor the bald clerk in uniform. Of course she was used to things being funny. Her uncle for a start. Then the place in Chester where they took her. Underneath the beds was empty; and the WC was in the house. A bit nasty that. At first.

Mrs. Oliphant sang alto in black before removals to Langham Hall where priests and nuns, all dressed like black crows with trailing wings, moved around her talking to her, as though she were merely a thing, taking her confessions in a little box like a coffin and telling her she was forgiven. And that seemed natural. They had given her prayers to say, assuring her that whatever she did and wherever she went and whatever happened to her she would always have beside her the Holy Mother. Maureen never really understood whose mother this had been, just knew, as soon as she saw the pale face, hooded like the cockle-woman from old Wirral above an infant, knew by the slope of her pale cheek and the star from heaven fastened always above her in the chapel, that this was her own mother made more useful by dying, made invisible except here, freed from the expense of needing to be fed so there should be more for her surviving children, more food, more clothes, more safety. The feeling was a continuation of what had been there before. And it was simple because it worked even when men spoke to her in the street, and took her. They were less real than Conrad but she shared her mother with them a bit, endured the rest like sleet for the comfort it brought Jim in the shape of 'his bottle.' *Has he had his bottle* had been her mother's last words to her, the 'he' in question being in those days her youngest brother, who had died before the war started, following her mother to St. Patrick's and sharing the same small stone. *Has he had his bottle* . . . the echo went on, freeing her from her aunt. Even her uncle's far-away eyes seemed to prove the validity of the instruction by reminding her of her infant brother's as he clasped his feed with the fanaticism of one, single love. They did now . . .

'God alive,' Jimmy managed. 'I won't say what I'm thinking.'

And his face became furrowed with a futile attempt to do the opposite. 'She could just look at a place like this . . .'

Suddenly he got help from a vision. He pointed at the wall. 'She was standing with several. You could smell 'em and hear 'em a mile off haw-hawing like a lot of sheep in winter . . . In grey top hats. I thought I'd said good-bye to her for ever, but of course not and I'll tell you why.'

His face lit as though he had struck by chance on a feeling better than booziness. ' "Jimmy," she said to me, "you've a lovely presence and if there's one thing I go for in a man it's presence. Cheerioh then, Jimmy, boy. And I'll be seeing you, just as soon as this bloody war is behind us or before." And now it's before; it's to-day. Maureen . . . what for did I get you back from evacuation? just to be bombed? just to read a picture paper and hang about the streets with people I'd be ashamed to know?'

He began to cry.

Maureen said, 'Stop it!'

'Well, then?' he said, and raised a handkerchief to his nose.

She loved him.

The noise of him had blended with the noise of traffic and the occasional hoot of tugs. He had always been there, always talking. He said the sirens were the angels weeping, and he talked with his arms out to Germany as though it were not a yard distant. Listening to him she'd thought all disaster was a mere game gone wrong which his own words put right. Heavens above, he said once, what a waste of light, when the whole docks were in flames. Yes, she loved him.

Even when he was unconscious she would go to his side to hear him whisper as he always did 'no bother at all.' He was like the Virgin, a great help.

He closed his eyes in the middle of a gesture.

'What for are you asking me . . .' he said gravely, 'go to the boy as we promised and give him a bite of food with the money mentioned . . . and . . . and . . .' his arm went out pleading for a little imagination, 'make him at home!'

Maureen lingered, staring.

'Now now . . . now now,' he said. 'Be off.'

Tim heard her coming.

He had not often been alone with a girl. The vicar at Garston had a daughter of his own age. Lucy. Every Christmas he was expected to entertain her for a whole afternoon. A

Python pelvis had been a help in 1939; and he always showed her the dungeon and the marks on the wall, said to have been left by the nails of prisoners in their dying convulsions. It gave him considerable pleasure shutting the door so that this vicar's daughter had to stand for a moment in the damp darkness, staring up till the tiny embrasure high above filtered through the disturbed optic purple of her innocent eyes, and made an impression on her of unattainable comfort. Poppy said he liked tormenting little girls, even her toddling daughters, one of whom did in fact still burst into tears whenever he appeared. 'Look! . . .' Poppy would say pointing at his face. '*He's delighted.*' And Tim, turning away, cursing, had to admit to a certain sense of pleasure. But how far was the annual orgy with Lucy from his father's gluttonous offer of 'priddy girls,' in America, and how little was it a preparation for this bizarre *tête-à-tête* with a scrofulous oik, wished upon him by Poppy. Perhaps nothing but his extreme and continuing resentment of Poppy and also now of Jakey enabled him to stand his ground, imagining as he did so that the female Cup would shortly be removed from him altogether when Maureen discovered his true feelings.

'Hallo,' she said behind him. 'They've gone!'

Tim drove the billiard cue forward so that the clash of the balls should answer her. But there was merely a rumbling and thumping of cushions as the missile careered round without connecting. If he was staying with one female he wished to make it clear that it was only out of revulsion from another.

'They've gone,' she repeated.

'Oh!' he said, stalking apathetically in pursuit of the dispersed balls.

'C'mon then,' she said, 'if you want yer dinner.'

A sort of panic came over him. He played several more inaccurate shots.

At last he put down the cue and prepared to follow her. She led him downstairs. They sat and she showed him a dirty card marked 'Tariff.'

'You can get fish and chips.'

He said, 'I thought we were eating at No. 42?'

'You got money from your father to eat 'ere, didn't you?' He shrugged and took the corner of the card. After a minute or two he said: 'It so happens he isn't my father.'

When he looked up he met her eyes . . . *feeding* on him.

Because she was thinking : *he's like Conrad!*

'Look . . . Anything wrong?' he said.

''Ow old are you, Tim?' she said.

And that was merely the beginning. From there she continued: Where did he live, why was he in Liverpool . . .

'Is it straight you're going to America?'

'Convoys tack, I understand.'

'Why are you going?'

'A weakness for the delights of tropical seas,' he said, becoming Bertie Wooster. 'Why d'you think?'

'Did you say tropical?' she said and then, 'Is *she going with you*?'

'Who's she: the cat's mother'? Echoes, even of nannies, stood in as substitutes for personal reactions. He was not far from panic, flight.

'Is she your sister then?'

'When exactly were you "bombed out"? ' he said trying to turn the tide.

'We weren't. 'Ave they *left* you then?' she complained.

'I ask nothing more,' he said.

'You what?' she said.

'Skip it.'

''Ow old *reelly* are you?'

'Look. *Do* you mind?'

Maureen stared at him, thinking of the tropic skies to which he was going. He had Conrad's aloofness. Conrad's silent strength.

When they had finished he paid two and six—waving aside a shilling of the change.

'Don't you want it?' she said.

'No.'

She thought, he's rich too: like Conrad.

The street was empty, the sky grey. The man at the counter looked at them. Tim looked at his watch in despair. Maureen said, 'Can you play snooker?'

There was no alternative.

She led the way back. On the stairs she caught his coat. He stopped dead, feeling fear at her touch.

'See that?' she said, and she pointed down.

He could see nothing.

'That stain.'

The light was feeble but by peering he could see a difference.

'Blood!' she said.

'What happened?' Tim obliged.

'Scrappin',' Maureen whispered. 'Bloke got killed.' She looked back down the stairs. '*Go on up*,' she added as though they might now be followed.

'I say, thanks awfully,' Tim said and he went on into the room. 'Murder, I presume,' he said facetiously.

'Are you sure you want to play?' she said.

'Can you suggest an alternative?' A moment later he said, '*What about* this "murder"? '

She walked away to get a cue.

'I never 'eard of any murder,' she said. 'And if I did I wouldn't go round shouting about it.'

He looked at her briefly. Apparently the conversation on the stairs had never happened.

They began snooker. After his first shot she said, 'Aren't you going to take yer coat off?'

'Oh. Yes,' he said listlessly as though his Dame had said, 'Loxley, aren't you going to do your shoes up.'

Then he changed his mind.

'In spite of your delightful fug,' he said, 'I think I won't.'

She considered him so intently that he said, 'Look! Have you seen a ghost?'

'You're like someone!' she said with sudden softness. 'Did you know that?'

'Frankly, no.'

22

'Are we right to leave Tim there?' Jakey said before starting the car.

'Safest place,' Poppy said, '*and* for the liddle old coat!'

She thought: he'd better know now.

He turned to look at her.

'Go on,' she said. 'Don't you want your little treat?'

'What coat?' he said.

'The one he's wearing.'

'It seemed to me a very ordinary coat!'

'That's what you think.'

And then she told him.

At first he sat there looking at her with a faintly quizzical expression as though on this occasion she had told a story too tall even to be funny. Plenty of early travellers had had a few sovereigns sewn into their clothing and it was typical of Bertrand's primitive nature that he should have followed their example; and typical of Poppy to turn it into the Crown Jewels. But something about her made him continue to stare . . . rather like a retriever at a tussock warned by its fleshy nose that a whole pheasant lay close.

'IT'S TRUE,' she said. 'Why d'you think I'm here? Charlie could have brought him.'

Jakey looked away up the street. He was rich enough to know the meaning of money.

'And he's wearing it now!' Jakey demurred.

'Well, of course.'

He felt as he did when a client revealed that all her savings were in St. Petersburg 3% Loan 1912. He made a limited movement with one hand.

'Hadn't we better go back *at once*.'

'Don't be an ass. You're worse than Bert,' and she gave a description of her husband's behaviour at King's Cross.

Jakey was bewildered.

'Why is he doing it?'

'An insurance policy . . . Perhaps a little bolt-hole pocket money for himself.'

Jakey was shocked—and doubtful. Bert had won a D.S.O. in the first war. Jakey was disinclined to believe those letters could ever be meaningless. To believe such a thing would be to take away a cornerstone from the careful architecture of his whole life. The very shoes he was wearing would depreciate perceptibly and immediately; also the way he carried himself at the wheel, in uniform, khaki or pin-stripe. Stowe and Christchurch would rock. John Buchan crumble. 'Whatever else he may be, Bert isn't a coward,' he said at last.

'*What* . . .' she cried. 'He'd get under the bed in air-raids if he wasn't so superstitious. But he thinks Someone Else is under there already.'

Jakey smiled unwillingly. 'It's true that he's seldom alone in a bedroom . . .'

'That's another thing. He complains about me, but it's nothing to what he does.'

Once started she could not stop. She just sat there in the creeping fog, her voice ribald, scoring off her absent husband.

Jakey was speechless with distaste.

Long years with his mother in Kensington had imposed upon him, almost without his noticing it, a Jekyll-Hyde personality as regards women. He had had affairs in the open, prolonged devotions to rich, chic women who were safely remote. He sent them notes in French, flowers, presents and gently bleeding love-letters. 'Poor old Jakey,' people laughed, 'hooked again.' But really these martyrdoms or troubadour attentions had something in common with his ineffective field sports. They made him feel he was doing the right thing. More: they meant invitations, even clients. But at the same time there had been a very few, very different affairs: a red-headed secretary, a penniless debutante, lately a Fanny driver. In these he had been effective, generous—and spent lavishly and with consideration, both during and after. Jardine-Matherson, he liked to think, would never have believed his success with women; and even they, the girls themselves, were surprised, entering his bed sometimes in a spirit of physical condescension, or maternal pity for his vulnerable shape and baby colouring; but leaving it flushed in every sense.

Even so he always put the light off, and never wrote to them. Poppy was the convergence of his two types of women into one. He wrote to her, pursued her with flowers, and had shared her bed. But so far only that. He looked at his watch.

'What's the matter with you?' Poppy demanded.

'Poppy dear. Go on.'

'What d'you mean "go on"?' she said angrily.

'About everything else except Bert.'

Poppy felt he hadn't understood. What else *was* there except Bert. His hand went out catching hers.

'Poppy,' he said. '*Go on!*'

'I've had enough of him . . .' she muttered, suddenly tearful.

The implied threat impressed him. Was this a prelude to a proposal? He did not remove his hand from hers, on the contrary clasped it tighter but not without a sense of pathos as though aware that he was inviting her to hurt him more than she would soon do anyhow. Never mind!

Poppy had no presentiments. She wanted sympathy, now.

'Even Charlie's had enough,' she said. 'He's joining up.'

Jakey loved Poppy more than ever for having to convict her husband via his chauffeur. To him this proved her complete sweetness. He looked sideways, prizing her proximity. Poppy! Clown, quadroon, M.F.H., Cleopatra, Florence Nightingale, Lucrezia Borgia . . . child.

How honoured he felt! How certain that he had not very long to enjoy her.

'*Mon petit chou!*' he said.

'Start the chou-chou.'

Of course he knew where his duty lay. 'Tim', he said. 'The coat!'

'They won't run away.'

He sat for a time. Oh, how he sat! At last he made one of his gestures, like a goggled pilot falling through an air-pocket, referring the crew to Nature for the explanation. Then they went.

As a frequenter of the Curzon Cinema and an admirer of Cocteau, all through the thirties, one of his papier-mâché dreams had been of pin-stripe elopement from a capitalist Gothic tower with some damsel distressed by a big bold steel baron. Instead, for years, he had returned nightly to 17 Queensgate Terrace.

So when Poppy suddenly said, 'I told him: I'll go somewhere else' it occurred to him that he had heard those very words before—spoken in the same rough tones. *From his mother referring to a tradesman.*

His face fell.

Luckily it had not far to fall.

And they held hands against the future, which meant he had to steer with only one.

In bed, without his spectacles, he looked blind and Poppy talked. Yes, Poppy who had brought him there so imperiously mocked her promise of 'a little treat' by continuing to *talk*, holding first his one hand and then the other, partly out of tenderness but partly also to frustrate or postpone their wanderings, which she soon objected were premature. In fact, Jakey was nothing if not patient. Poppy started on Peter—the Phantoms. Soon Jakey found himself looking at the ceiling and finding it harder and harder to concentrate sufficiently on what his divine woman was saying in order to provide the answers she wanted to hear. Several times in this respect he failed her utterly, simply through physical preoccupation. Finally he came wearily back to dialogue whereupon his state of preparedness subsided. Noticing this she took pleasure in deriding him. 'God,' she said. 'What was all the fuss about?'

Of course he knew by now that you couldn't do right with Poppy. At moments the only consolation in being in bed with her was the thought of all the important people who wanted to be and weren't. But he was man enough to find this a limited kick. He got more from the feeling that she couldn't do without him, even if she couldn't do much with him. Yes, this touched him deeply, turning everything into good. Her very garrulity, even when it was the last thing he wanted, proved that he, like his journey, was really necessary.

And so he lay, while she snuggled against him talking, presuming on his total agreement with one mad generalisation after another. A funny form of sex. Just when he was despairing she fell silent and began to rub the palm of one of his hands with a little circular motion, and sometimes pressing it. This was the signal. He knew that he must not refer to it as such however deviously or even respond to it at once; knew also he must not speak of what was going to happen, because on one level at least 'it' disgusted and humiliated her. Who knows why? Perhaps for such a rough rider to be ridden, the inclinations of her uppermost defensive nature had first to be obliterated or reversed. Even then there were problems. When she abandoned attempts to dominate, she became more childlike than feminine; could easily become tear-stained, clutching, the very soaked opposite of lusty. Oh, he had to go carefully! Only this little movement of one of her hands and her averted face and a rather dreamy look in her eyes accompanied by ever more extreme and nonsensical evaluation of her husband told him that now at last, like Barkis, she was moderately mad and therefore willing. But what, by now, about him?

Jakey was always resilient in this field. A touch, a caress, an inhalation of hair and a long look at the charming nape, the slender body, the breasts, pear-shaped like the full udders of a goat, the proud line of her extraordinary profile and the rims of those vast, touching eyes which seemed to know so much more than she could ever have said even if she'd had the benefit of even primary education—thickened the blood again quickly and produced a firm limb which for some reason was more athletic than his other four put together.

'Poppy,' he said, and put his lips to hers with the gentle tactile thirst of one who has waited too long. Sweet salivation immediately gave him the feeling that he was drinking her divine love . . .

The telephone rang.

He rolled away slowly as though in his sleep.

'You'd better take it,' he said. He looked dazed.

Poppy stretched across a naked arm which immediately roughened into goose-flesh. He kissed it underneath: A crumb from beneath some sort of table. Duff was looking at him, offended.

'Yupp?' Poppy said aggressively.

Her face fell—and she covered the mouthpiece as though putting out a fire. 'It's Bert!'

Jakey closed his eyes and Poppy's whole weight came down

on his chest as though he were a table. Her eyes seemed to forget his existence and see Bert's instead.

'Wal, wal,' she said. 'And how are yooooo?'

Bert's voice, reduced by electronics to raucous sibilance, was plainly audible to Jakey. He wanted to know if there was any more news of the convoy. Disappointed in this, he wanted to speak to Tim.

'You can't . . . He's downstairs playin' around.'

'Well, ring down for him.'

'It's a big hotel.'

'Page him—I want to speak to the little blighter.'

'O.K. He'll ring you back,' Poppy said.

'O.K. How's the life-jacket?'

'Okedoke,' she said.

'Locked up?'

'Right under my nose.'

'Good girl . . . hm . . .' His voice dropped to a sultry sexy intimate note. 'Missing me?' he said.

She managed a compromise note.

'Rather lonesome in Liverpuddle,' she drawled.

'I want my little Popsy here,' he said in a gluey voice. 'Right here . . . gotta liddle place for you right here.'

'Keep it warm,' she said.

Jakey heard the sound of a kiss like someone pulling off a plaster. He closed his eyes. Then came the clank of the receiver. They lay in silence.

'We've got to get him,' she said. 'And quick!'

Jakey saw a look in her face which he had seen before. Fear of Bertrand. Perhaps, who knows, the same emotion had drawn her to marry the man in the first place—just as it drew her to hunters high as a house, slums rabid with poverty.

'That's the second time he's rung up to-day,' she accused.

'He's anxious.'

'Nuts you mean.'

She got out of bed. Jakey put on his spectacles and she turned from recent Picasso to an Ingres. He was feeling disappointed, *au fond.*

Poppy was at her face. 'God! What's the fuss?' she exclaimed. 'He's with Jimmy, isn't he?'

He realised she was talking to Bert. Nevertheless he answered.

'Yes, he's with Jimmy.'

At that moment the sirens started up. At first low, almost caressing . . .

Then the full music.

They both became motionless as they looked up at the misty roof-tops.

'Here, too!' Poppy objected. She turned to look at him as though he ought to be able to prevent it.

'Yes,' he said and put his legs out into the cold. His socks were attached to suspenders which glimmered so he was able to locate them without difficulty. But he had no wish to put them on. Only the thought of Tim and a sure sense of what a gentleman would do enabled him to persevere.

Even so he put one hand to his heart. Soon, he felt, it would hurt.

'What's up?' she rapped out.

He pretended to be scratching.

23

Tim and Maureen were like one of those gadgets in the window of an optician, an infinitely slow perpetuum mobile of two agents round a fixed centre, a neat materialisation of time. They spoke hardly at all to each other though Tim's frequent exclamations of 'God' or 'Christ' after the click of balls, might not have occurred had he been alone. She, for her part, found her hair an obstruction: it flopped over one eye whenever she bent down to play which meant she had to free that side of her face with a slow movement of one hand which Tim couldn't help looking at. Then she'd tap the ball gently where she wanted it to go, which was in all respects a change from him. When she had caressed the black out of sight he exploded:

'God.'

His tone was full of his predicament. Billiard rooms were familiar. At Garston, when he was not reading or with Charlie in the garage, he was often in the billiard room, playing fives or doing his bones on a dust-sheet. The natural continuation of those days, emerging from the infinity of childhood, was that here and now, since he was in a billiard room, it should belong to a hypothetical Lord Liverpool and that in a moment, since it was getting dark, Charlie would be announced ready with a bearskin rug over one arm to take him home through wintry lanes. The fact that his next journey was to be outward, as it were through that vast grey window which he had seen in the hotel, out into the most certain emblem of Nowhere that he had ever seen, added an edge of his tone, when he gave tongue to his affronted vanity.

'I suppose,' he drawled, 'that if I owned a billiard saloon and had damn all else to do 365 days per year I might beat you rather easily.'

She said, 'I don't own it,' but he smiled as though he had beaten her with his words, if not with his cue.

'It's my cousin's,' she said.

This too gave him an opportunity. He prolonged his smile, deliberately suggesting that the idea of her having a cousin, in the same sense that he had cousins, was somewhat humorous.

'Who on earth is your cousin?' he said.

'Lou Cochrane!'

The meaningfulness of her tone suggested she had said Clark Gable.

It was another opportunity: 'Who ON EARTH is Lou Cochrane?' he derided. And to rub the joke in he repeated, before playing a shot out of turn, 'Lou Cochrane!' He miscued—so said, 'Possibly Lou Cochrane might consider buying some new cues.'

'Tell him,' she said.

Tim said: 'I suppose he was here when the "bloke" got killed on the stairs.'

He spoke as a J.P. and sloped round the table after his ball, smiling grimly at the sort of relations she probably had. Before playing he glanced up at her. She was standing dead opposite, under the faint lights, like a target at the other end of his extended weapon, not answering.

'Christ!' he said, and played another bad shot.

'Why d'you take the name of the Lord?' she said.

'Look, isn't it your turn?'

She didn't move as though snooker were now over.

'A' you liking it 'ere, Tim?'

'If you're going to turn this into a quiz . . . ! I came here to play billiards.'

'You ain't much good.'

He slammed the ball hard. He was playing by himself now.

'You'd do a lot better if you took your coat off for a start.'

'I think I'll keep it on if you don't mind.'

'Got 'oles in your shirt?'

'My shirt is virtually new.'

'Boy in Chester wouldn't show his feet . . . Know why? 'E 'adn't got any toes!'

Tim took off his coat, twanged his braces and puffed out his chest.

'There!'

''Ang it up,' she said, not impressed.

There were three pegs, one with the hanger.

'What are you?' she said.

'What d'you mean?'

'Inches round the chest? I'd a friend did these exercises with springs. 'E was forty.'

'My dear girl,' Tim said. 'I haven't the foggiest.'

She looked at him attentively as though he had three ears.

'You're not like other boys, are you?'

'And I suppose you think . . .'

At that moment there was a bang and the door opened. Two men came in. One was small with a lean hatchet face and the other unusually large. The small one was smoking a cigar and looked like a gangster in a film, and the big one like a bishop at an important service, except for his clothes and the fact that he only had one ear.

They nodded and the small one said 'Maureen' and looked at Tim as though he were a German spy. Tim was thankful to have been spared the intimacies of a hungry, unwashed female but not elated by the appearance of the newcomers. Removing his thumbs from his braces he turned back to the table as though that and that only explained his presence here. 'I rather think,' he said in his most Woosterish manner, 'that the moment has come to push on' and so saying he struck the ball in such a way that it hopped cleanly over its target and even the edge of the table.

The two men were hanging up their coats. They looked at the rolling ball and then at him again.

Maureen went to pick up the ball. Passing Tim she whispered: 'Lou.'

It was at this moment that the sirens began to wail.

Both the newcomers stared resentfully at the ceiling.

'Fucken listen to that!' said the small one. He had black elastic round his biceps, like garters.

'Not fucken four o'clock!' the bishop protested.

They all stood still, listening as though on a November 11th service. But no sound of gun or aircraft came.

The pale man from the coffee-bar came up and put up the black-outs. The two men spoke to him in low tones, and the small one looked at Tim as though he had done something he shouldn't have done, something very, very serious.

At that moment there was a shriek cut-off in its prime by a shattering explosion. The whole building seemed to take a pace back and they staggered as though they were on a ship. Then the lights went out.

Tim heard in the dark: 'I'm fucken out of here.'

Then he heard a woman screaming in the street. The sound came and went and there was a confusion of voices, but no alteration to this woman's wail. Tim seemed to have heard the sound before. And this made it more awful as though for years it had been maturing inside him, becoming always more awful and had now jumped from cover. He wanted something to *kill it!* Quickly!

For a few seconds the sound was obliterated by other

explosions and he heard Maureen say: 'That's guns in the playgrounds.' She was quite close.

Tim heard footsteps and the voice of the short man, then Maureen, close, her voice as though she were remembering something that had happened long ago.

'It's just guns like.'

The scream altered, became muffled.

Lights flickered on the stairs, outlining legs. Then the pale man's face welled up with an oil lamp below it, floating slowly up like a Chinese lantern at a festival.

'Mr. Cochrane . . .' he inquired, looking round, 'Mr. Cochrane . . .'

He came into the room rotating, and saw them.

'It's in Hope Street,' he said with a sort of sickly confidence. 'Where's Mr. Cochrane?'

He put down the lamp.

'I had the light ready . . .' he said.

But there was no Mr. Cochrane, no one except the two children.

'They've gone,' Maureen said. 'Their coats have gone, see.'

Tim saw and went up to the remaining one, touching it.

'Christ,' he said.

'What's up now?' she said.

He lifted the imposter coat and thumped it. 'That's not mine . . . One of those clots has taken mine.'

Maureen didn't want to hear, not in front of the pale man holding the lamp.

Tim put the strange coat on as though this would be sufficient to restore it to a proper identity or put an end to optical illusions. His hands which had slipped into the pockets came out aghast—with a small square automatic.

'Put it away,' Maureen whispered, stepping between him and the light.

Tim felt funny all over at the cold dead weight in his palm.

He had touched real automatics before, even fired one. But this . . . this felt different, *alive*, like a snake or something. He took the coat off and Maureen hung it up.

The pale man waited.

'We're going,' she said.

Tim put on his overcoat and sloped after her: 'Would you,' he said in the dark, 'kindly now take me immediately to the house of the moron who relieved me of my coat. If the said Mr. Cochrane *is* your cousin there should be no difficulty. Moreover I feel a shade chilly and so would you . . .' and so on and on, pursuing her with words along the dark pavement, following the vague outline of her slender figure, clasping his enormous lack about him.

She was in nothing but her dress, a thin dress, and the wind blew through it but she was already telling her uncle or her aunt in advance. We never met those two. We met two other people. And we never saw no gun.

24

The electricity main which fed Light Street also fed the Alhambra. The same darkness which deprived Tim of his coat separated Jakey from his trousers—a loss that could not be compared had not the neat officer been shocked, in mid-search, by a knock on the door and a voice from behind it offering light. He shot into a cupboard while Poppy called 'Come in.' That was not all. She had to call him out before the maid was properly clear of the room. The maid must have heard.

'Poppy . . .' he began.

'Do me up,' she said. She was standing still as a statue in front of the mirror. Candles both in front and to one side made her look more fetching than ever. The long V at the back of her dress was open down to the *naissance des fesses*, an area which always arrested him as much, though differently, as similar slopes in front. He put a hand there reverently and another on the rivals.

'Je t'aime,' he murmured—so quietly that he had to put his lips more or less into her ear . . . and then his tongue.

She jibbed and said, 'Look: hook me up, then zip me up . . .' and she took his hands off as though they were a couple of old poultices. Habits are tyrants and the absence at this moment of her lady's-maid made her short-tempered. He began to try to help.

'What *are* you doing? . . . If it's broken, say so.'

The King's oculist had decreed the density of his spectacles but even a young watchmaker, he thought, with his special glass, could not have found the eye to this brassière-hook in light softer than that of a low harvest moon.

'It *is* broken,' he decided.

'Well I don't need the thing,' she said and shrugged out of it and the top part of her dress. The boast was justified. But to go without a customary garment, one of the 39 articles, so to speak, of decency, struck Jakey as an invitation to the kind of disaster to which he could not put a name. 'Poppy darling,' he protested. 'We're going out . . .'

He watched the movement in the lovely long groove of her back from behind and in the mirror saw the sudden jollification in front—as she did away vigorously with the two nests of *broderie anglaise*. It was too much. Candlelight seemed to add the desire of ancestors to his own now. How much he had had to do without came home to him hard. 'Poppy . . .' he begged. Because really he could have eaten her. Wild gigantic shadows made her religious. Apocalypse raged outside. He wanted to celebrate the High Mass of life. 'Poppy,' he said beginning to go after her, 'won't you be cold?'

'Later,' she said.

In time he sat down again to the hand-made shoes. He could see their style.

Even when there has been a clearly defined climax, there is something crude and loveless about dressing together immediately after recently undressing together. Love, it seems, should have at least a snooze afterwards. And as for the thwarting of love . . . Jakey was bruised. He regarded a dressing-room as a minimal requisite of co-habitation, even in war-time.

She talked. To herself, really.

He was schooling himself to what hadn't happened, protesting to himself that so far he had enjoyed nothing but a long monologue in the nude about Bertrand, when suddenly the telephone rang.

Poppy said, 'You're the nearest . . . It'll just be Tim.'

'It may not be,' he said firmly.

Seeing the futility of insistence and remembering his retreat to the cupboard she made her way to the instrument.

'Hallo,' she said roughly. '. . . Oh! You again!'—and she raised mocking eyebrows, indicative of Bert, at Jakey.

The wire crackled. Poppy's face sagged and wilted. She covered the mouthpiece and whispered, 'He knows you're here . . . and he knows Tim's out.'

'O.K. O.K.,' she said wearily. 'But I tell you he's fine; he's with a friend . . . what? An old friend, Jimmy Lennox, racehorse trainer. Yupp . . . Out in the suburbs . . . Sure, there's a raid. That's why he's better there than here. Here, we're in the thick of it . . . Well, he got it wrong. It's right here. In front of my eyes.' She looked up at Jakey, shook her head and closed her eyes to signify madness. He queried with his eyes. She covered the mouthpiece and while Bert spoke on to himself whispered, 'The hall porter told him which coat Tim had on.' She sat down enduring the onslaught. 'To-night!' she suddenly cried. 'You're crazy, darling . . . but you won't get a train will you?' then defeated, 'O.K.—he's right here . . .'

'He wants to speak to you.' She held out the receiver.

'To *me* . . .'

'Yes!'

Jakey still held back.

'*Take it!*'

Jakey obeyed. 'Bertrand,' he said. After all they had shot together, played cards . . . always acknowledged each other in the houses of mutual friends, though not at Ascot. Still, there was no precedent for a correct tone. So Jakey waited for a lead—and heard geniality.

'At least I can count on you,' Lord Bewick began.

This confused Jakey, further.

'Now, Jakey,' Lord Bewick went on in his charm voice, a special stop of his as easily recognisable as low gear in a car. 'I hear Poppy's let Tim go off with his life-jacket . . . Do you know what I mean?'

Jakey left him in doubt.

'Hallo?' said Lord Bewick a little louder, revealing strain.

'Hallo,' said Jakey.

'Look! I know . . . I know how it is. This is the point: You're an officer. You've got batteries up there. Transport. Influence . . . Hallo?'

'But Bertrand . . .'

'Hallo.' Bertrand's charm had cracked. Now his tone changed, becoming tougher with every word. 'I want you to get Tim back at once from wherever he is, hallo—and keep an eye on everything till I arrive . . . I can rely on you. *I'm glad you're there* . . . Hallo . . . *Hallo?*'

Jakey was speechless. Bertrand's tone was that of a general to a captain or a chairman to an executive. And man to man. *On the same side.*

A voice interrupted: the line was needed. Bertrand objected strongly. The voice insisted. Lord Bewick exploded into passionate assertion of his identity, his office and the priority nature of the call which had been arranged for him. 'Operator, operator—let me speak to the superintendent. This is Lord Bewick . . .' There followed a debate. The participants appeared to be drawn from all over Britain.

Jakey was patriotically shocked. The precarious tenet of his professional faith as a stockbroker had been that the *privacy* of some operations was justified by being the *sine qua non* of *gentlemen*, a category which had been outlined and emphasised again and again from Sir Philip Sydney to Cardinal Newman and which, to him, as a half foreigner, contained a semi-religious significance, the very elixir, even in 1940, of England's survival, witness such men as Douglas Bader and Richard Hillary and the neatness with which he had just done up his left shoe, and would soon have done up his other. Yes, all had some bearing on this issue; as indeed did Poppy whose presumptions, in his eyes, were all wonderful, like the guns of the *Revenge*, which he had sung of at Stowe. He took off his spectacles, as though Bertrand had suddenly postulated a new way of looking at almost everything under the hotel chandelier (designed for gas) a way which made it necessary to be blind.

'Bertrand,' he said as soon as the debate ended. 'I'm in an invidious position.'

'You're in a *what*?' Bertrand was always annoyed by jargon.

Jakey couldn't go on down that road. He cocked his head up and saw Poppy shake her head.

'Refuse,' Poppy said.

Jakey had no idea what she meant. But apparently Bert did for he shouted, 'I'm just asking you to keep an eye on my boy. *Are you refusing?*'

After a long moment Jakey said, 'I'll do that if I can for Tim, Bertrand. Good-bye,' and he put down the receiver.

He stood up, wishing he hadn't been in his shirt-sleeves.

Poppy wanted him to repeat every word, but he was too disgusted. And confused. Paradoxes inherent in his position as a gentleman Catholic stockbroker sleeping with Lady Bewick had always been amenable to a little manipulation along the lines of the classical golden mean. But Poppy always precipitated the sort of extreme *confrontations* which it was the sole purpose of civilisation to mitigate. She was really impossible.

He said, 'You've made me his . . . cat's-paw.'

'I *what*?'

She considered him, with that tragic clown's face. He had to turn from it to make his protest possible.

Then suddenly she began laughing, helplessly.

'Poppy, *stop!*' he commanded.

She made herself laugh more.

But he wouldn't—*couldn't* have it. His only comfort lay in treating his position as a rescue operation—for the boy. This approach at least was familiar; it was like investing for an orphan. He was in charge. So he must know what he had to deal with.

'Now let's do things properly,' he said.

'*What* . . .'

'Where did you *meet* this . . . Lennox?'

She began to laugh helplessly. And suddenly he was frightened of her, as he had been when he first met her . . . as he had been when she put him on Cavalier, just to see him being bolted with.

'I asked a quite straightforward question, Poppy darling. I want to get things straight . . .'

An explosion, not very far away, supported him, perhaps, in the tone he had adopted—but brought the conversation to an end, demanding action not words.

25

Tim called to Maureen who was ahead in the dark. She waited for him to come up.

'I'd have you know,' he said, 'that I've lost my coat.'

'Well, I'm not stayin' in there,' she said.

She got to a door. They looked up, hearing a soft *mou-mou-mou* high up in the sky. Ack-ack shells winked like fireworks that have failed to develop and the long beams of the search-lights crossed each other or were blunted by clouds. They were like the funnelled light of suns in reverse.

Tim forgot his coat and began to take heady pleasure from the sheer violence of the sounds. Each explosion made the coat seem less important. He had been lost anyhow; the coat had merely followed suit. The gulping, shattering guns endorsed his sense of exalted indifference. Colossal din and even risk seemed suddenly a liberation, keys to his case.

In the west a seam of luminous shells chased each other, lazily, out to sea.

Maureen said, 'That's the Navy.'

They heard a far crescendo whine followed by a series of explosions, and great flashes of light so brief there was no time to take in what they showed. The children stood looking back with their lips parted. Fire glow behind chimneys. It was unreal, magnificent, not dangerous at all. The recent screams of pain, the ambulance and rescue work going on at the end of the road, belonged to the humdrum world of other people but this all round and up there was for them and larger, more wonderful than reality.

Maureen said: 'It's less'n last time.'

Miss Lennox opened the door to them.

A single blade of flame in a glass funnel beneath the hat-stand threw its prongs into weird relief as though revealing the presence of some colossal unseen stag. They heard a voice calling.

'It's Uncle Tom,' Miss Lennox said as though Maureen were to blame.

'Is he all right?' Maureen said.

'Are you going to the shelter then, Maureen . . . ?'

Miss Lennox looked at Tim, trying to take him in.

'By the way . . .' he began. 'It's probably not the slightest interest but . . .'

Maureen said, 'Upstairs,' and pushed him.

Miss Lennox looked at her niece dismissing her utterly. She said to Tim:

'Does you mother know you're still here, Sir?'

'He's to stay with Uncle Jimmy,' Maureen claimed.

Miss Lennox considered them both. Then she pointed at Maureen. 'Mrs. Oliphant for you,' she said. 'To-morrow. I've had enough.'

'Mrs. Elephant,' Maureen said.

'Well, you're not staying here, not doing as you like!'

Tears stood in her eyes. Maureen yelled. 'Mrs. Elephant's joined up. Father Doyle told me and I ain't going back to Chester even if you carry me. He said I needn't. Ask him . . .'

By then her aunt had gone back in towards the voice and shut the door.

'You don't know where I can get a cab by any chance, do you?' Tim said.

'You want your coat?' she said.

'How?' he said sarcastically. 'What plan would you suggest?'

'Pray, I should.' She went up.

'I sincerely hope your uncle has a more reliable suggestion.'

They were on the stairs and she turned again and looked at him as though he had fallen out of that quaking lurid sky beyond the walls and alighted here at her feet. He could see she kept expecting something.

'Do you mind proceeding,' he said.

'What's that?' she said, still standing.

'I'd like to have a word with your uncle?'

She gave way, led him up and opened a door on the landing.

A candle stuck in a bottle showed Jimmy Lennox lying on his bed. The whisky bottle was empty on its side.

'Apples,' he whispered.

They went close and saw he had not been speaking to them. There were flakes at the corners of his mouth and the stud-hole of his shirt was frayed over white stubble.

Maureen turned to Tim as much as to say 'Well? There's your coat!'

Tim hailed the far-away man: 'Hallo there, Mr. Lennox!'

Jimmy seemed to have heard. Reaction coalesced in his eyes. He put out an adamant hand and said, 'A friend of Mr. Hickling is no friend of mine.'

'MR. LENNOX,' Tim shouted. 'Where can I find MR. LOU COCHRANE.'

Jimmy closed his bleary eyes with an expression of refined distaste, raising his right index finger to his pursed lips and holding it here in a vertical position.

Maureen trailed away into the shadows. She was vast on one wall. Tim said to her:

'Then tell me how I can return to the hotel.'

She was lighting another candle.

Tim stared mutinously at his surroundings, as though it were some daft theatrical at Garston Women's Institute run by mad Poppy.

'You don't understand actually,' he said; and noticed something funny about his own voice.

Maureen stared. Enormous eyes! She's entirely crackers, Tim thought.

But, she was merely seeing him all the time, more and more, as Conrad. The face was the same.

'It's not just the coat,' he said.

'Did you leave money in it?' she said.

She visualised a green pound or perhaps a brown ten shillings. She understood.

Tim turned away from her violently and slumped in a chair. His emotions had no shape. He felt, as he sat there, about as drunk as Lennox. Where was he? His thoughts began to race. One moment he felt, 'Good! Perhaps it will teach them!' The next: 'What have I done?'; heard voices, 'Loxley, you'll lose your head next.' 'If you can't do it right first time, you'd better do it again.' 'I wonder what they'll think of you over there.' 'You'll be the Earl of Bewick instead of me. Good luck!' 'Just a liddle guy with a liddle coat cast on the ocean wave' and Poppy's fingers on his flesh. Then that window, vast, grey, shapeless. A dopey feeling spread over him. He twisted his head this way and that, rubbed his nose, and swore.

'I mean, *is* he your cousin or isn't he?'

'They'll come soon,' Maureen said.

'Well, they bloody well better,' Tim said.

A plaintive note had arrived in his voice.

Jimmy said: 'He was sweet as summer . . .'

Mou-mou-mou above.

Tim's eyes strayed up to the ceiling as though to see through it.

Where? . . . why . . . ?

Maureen had gone behind the screen. He could see her bending and looking under the bed, dragging out heaven knows what noisome totem of oik female privacy. He stared fascinated, waiting. Sure enough she made a find, considered it and then came towards him. His heart beat faster, as though soon it would start, the real stuff, like that woman in the Edgware Road. What else could you expect. Still she came nearer—the guns shook the house as though it were a crate. He almost cried out to her to keep away, as he had to Poppy, by his bed. But she was holding some sort of magazine printed on newspaper. 'Here,' she said and pointed to a face. 'That's you, innit?'

He saw a chap with a turned-up nose and a row of teeth like a piano keyboard peering down from a height of two inches at a girl with eyelashes like the legs of a big spider.

Above was written: *Conrad finds Lana tied to the ground.* She bent forward and whispered, 'It is, you know!'

'Look . . .' Tim said but he couldn't finish, couldn't bring out the usual snub, just pushed the thing away.

Maureen dropped the comic in his lap. But he wouldn't look at it, or even touch it, because she had put it there.

Time passed in the form of noise.

His eyes gravitated to the white-hot wick of the lamp.

The protecting glass was supported at the base by a brass collar made of small flimsy fleur-de-lis. One or two of these were broken and held his gaze, till his eyes drifted out of focus in the vacant centre of light. Time flickered long shadows down centuries, merged now naturally with the noise of the guns and presence of Jimmy and Maureen. It was as though he had mislaid himself, like a pocket-knife of last holidays, and the flame found him, blurring the boundaries of his identity till he stood in need of them no more than when he was asleep. Which he almost was: everything round about like long ago, two faces shadowy as skulls, surfaces dull as fallen leaves, shadows moving slowly like weeds in the stream where he used to play boats as a child at Garston. Maureen might have been seeing the same memory so like was her expression to his, as she gazed at the gently moving flame.

'What was it in the coat then?' she said. 'Because if Lou found it you can say goodbye to it . . .'

The boy looked at her resentfully—as though *mirages* had no right to speak. Then explosions went some way to proving her reality. Still, he didn't answer.

'Tim,' she said with more confidence, sensing in this relationship some of the agreeable superiority which she enjoyed over her uncle. 'What was in it . . . you 'avn't said.'

'Jewels,' he said.

She knew then: he *was* Conrad.

It took a moment or two to digest.

And Lana said to him 'I can help you Conrad.' 'How can you help me?' he said, 'you're just a girl.' 'I know the lagoon,' she said, 'it's my home.'

'What?' Tim said.

She hadn't spoken but lowered her eyes. The Conrad-story had a happy end. The Mother of God always sent happy ends. She answered you, so Maureen had put four petitions in the box at the back of St. Peter's. All for Conrad to come. Each had been bought with the left-overs of proceeds from ten-minute stands with sailors against warehouse walls. The main went for Jimmy's bottle. First things first. Now she wanted Tim to get his coat, like Jimmy got his bottle. Her face became quite a board meeting. The virgin would bless them and together they would go away like Conrad and Lana to live happy ever more. But what would happen to Jimmy? Who would give him his bottle? She wanted to give everyone everything. Her sombre eyes lit with faith in the possibility of so doing. After all, her mother had done it. She remembered her mother doing it. Every day.

A fog-horn mourned suddenly. The sound was familiar to her as the sight of gulls on masts, derricks in mist. Coming as it did in a lull of explosions it was reassuring as the face of a friend in a crowd. So were her uncle's snores, though each sounded like the last noise he'd ever make. And Conrad had said, 'Jewels' . . . Not Conrad really at all. A stranger whom she would never see again. Her fingers strayed to the cross at her neck while she looked at him. A raid was passing, an opportunity slipping by. He made her feel inadequate, almost indecent by his neglect of the uses to which others put her, whether against the wall or on the ground. Here there was even a bed. Raids made men pay more, and do it more. Because they might wake up in heaven where it wasn't done.

'You said jewels,' she said. ''Ow many?'

Tim got a heady feeling, a desire to put himself in a proper perspective, long overdue.

'Only about a million pounds sewn into the lining.'

She said: 'You know at first I believed you. You said it so natural like.'

'Look . . . !' he said angrily.

'Are you in with Lou, then . . . ?' she teased.

'Look, just you get my coat; I'll wait here.'

He got up restlessly.

She considered him. There was something in the coat! After all.

'I suppose you wouldn't 'elp much, would you, even if you did come.'

He shrugged. 'He's not *my* cousin.'

Maureen wondered at him. ''Ave you ever been in a fight?' she said.

'No.'

'What '*ave* you done?' she said.

His desire to escape from her rendered him speechless.

'Come 'ere,' she said, 'no—come on—closer.

'Touch me . . .' she said. 'Go on. *Kiss me!*

'Are you funny, then?' she said.

Tim would have liked to . . . liked . . . he would have liked to . . . and he stood there thinking I *will*, now I really *will* . . . and he stood there, knotted inside himself deciding: this time she really has asked for it. Meaning murder.

'Well, are you?' she said.

'I'm not MAD keen to catch leprosy,' he burst out.

She stared into his face a moment, then she turned, and went to the door. 'C'mon then,' she said. 'If you want to.'

After a moment's hesitation Tim said, 'Oh, for Christ's sake,' and followed.

They went next door.

The billiard room was dark. Maureen's torch beam moved along the coat hooks; halting at the end—on a single coat-hanger.

'It's gone,' Maureen said.

The pale man behind the café counter said from the stairs: 'Lou came back.'

'Did he leave the other coat?' Maureen said.

The pale man shrugged. Apparently he had never heard of anyone called Lou.

They went through the musty black-out curtain, smelling of old fry.

'So what's the programme now?' Tim demanded and rapped the door post with his knuckles. The idea of getting into a taxi and saying 'Hotel Alhambra' was the only one that made any sense.

But Maureen said 'C'mon.'

26

The swing-doors of the Alhambra were turning fast to let people in when Poppy and Jakey went out.

Sky in the west was still light blue. Poppy said, 'Not much doin',' and stood for a moment looking up, disappointed. Jakey took her arm as though she were a child getting cold. She said Light Street was only half a mile 'if we don't go round the town first.'

An air of expectancy affected the way people walked, as it affects children after the start of a game of hide and seek. Poppy, even in the car, kept peering up and making sensational conjectures so that before they had gone very far Jakey felt he had already survived several near misses. In fact, the bangs in question were all distant gun-fire. He begged to be spared her commentary: finding Light Street by day had been hard enough, now, in the gloaming, it would depend on whether or not he could pick up the silhouette of the public baths. 'Ask,' she said. He stopped by a white-helmeted policeman—who didn't know, having come from Chester that afternoon. 'What's happening in Chester?' Poppy called, leaning across, as if they were all three at the theatre.

Jakey drove her away unanswered. He was rather silent. Responsibility for Tim and the anomaly of his own position at the wheel, searching for Lord Bewick's diamonds, made him peer coldly and professionally into the various optical illusions which offered themselves as roads.

But a sudden flash and explosion made him put out a hand in a rather French gesture, like a porter proved right in some branch of pessimism particularly dear to him.

Poppy said, 'Better than a day's hunting.'

'Please!' he said.

Making the best of a bad job was one thing; slap-happy garrulity another. Besides, the sheer technical problem of finding Light Street provided him with the priority of work. Only when Poppy began to attack her husband for his 'cock-eyed obsession with the coat' did he feel bound to point out that such an attitude was 'a good deal more realistic' than what she had done.

For someone who spent her life breaking rules Poppy's reaction to blame was astonishingly fresh. She now heaped abuse on her critic: he was so conventional that he expected people to steal merely because they were hungry; he wanted to keep Tim in Eton collars till he was seventeen 'like your aunt did you, ticking off the times you went to the lavatory after breakfast till you were thirty'—he made another gesture but she kept coming, like the German aircraft.

'A little more Light Street,' she said, 'might do you and Tim a lot of good.'

He made yet another gesture, for his own satisfaction, a sort of circular wave—to evoke, in the name of sanity, the foamy sheepskin rug (since she must talk about a lavatory) which she regarded as a *sine qua non* for her own feet whenever she went to that place; also the muslin bag of lavender and rose-leaves weighting the delicate fan of toilet paper without which her intestines felt shy.

'*Je t'en prie, chérie*,' he murmured. 'I must find this street.'

Suddenly a figure with a white armband loomed in front.

'Picking up a child,' Jakey shouted, 'Light Street?'

The man waved him on, shouting, 'If it's still there.'

Roofs on one side suddenly shone as though in sunlight.

'God!' Poppy said.

'There's a moral in this,' Jakey said. '. . . If I could find it.'

'You'd be doing better if you found the chimney.

'Light Street!' Poppy suddenly cried, like someone saying 'House!' in a lottery. He asked her not to shout. She claimed he would have gone past it 'like a mole' if she hadn't.

At the far end they could see vehicles and an ambulance.

'You see!' Jakey said.

The windows of No. 42 were dead. As they got out their voices were drowned by a salvo from close A.A. guns. Stuff rattled on the road like hail. Poppy moved into the wall.

'Guns,' Jakey said.

'Better get out your Hamlyn Toob!'

She began laughing, silently, her eyes glistening; she was possessed by a curious exultation which his solemnity aggravated.

He knocked. But while he was knocking the guns seemed to put feet through the rotten floorboards of the sky. He looked at her, his spectacles gleaming.

The door remained shut. Poppy looked through the letter box and saw a candle. 'Hoy,' she yelled through the slot.

'You'll be arrested.'

'Quit bleating . . .' She had a go at the door-knocker and Jakey thought she was the loudest woman he had ever known. He told her people went to shelters during raids. They argued. But coherent thought, such as a man makes use of to win an argument, is something like riding a bicycle, a matter of perpetual balance and progress. Noise beyond a given number of decibels can make it impossible. Several times Jakey tried to think of things to say to Poppy which would bring her to her senses but at the last moment they were jolted off course. Still for once he wanted to 'win,' wanted to crush her feckless, flippant assertion that she was blameless. Because with every passing moment he became more and more concerned for the missing boy—and ashamed of his own negligence. He must have been blind, deaf, dumb. Why? Because of her. In a sense she was destroying him, a process which he might have enjoyed in other circumstances; but not now, not here.

She began climbing on to the window ledge.

'Poppy, darling . . . Must you?'

The A.A. guns extinguished him. When they stopped she was talking.

'. . . What did I tell you . . .'

The door was opening. Soon it showed half Jimmy's face in candlelight, a face in mid-vision.

'Who's that?' he said.

'Wakey, wakey,' Poppy crowed. Jakey helped her down.

Jimmy made way for her though his bleary face remained dull and unrecognising.

The candle flickered wildly in the draught. They went in and closed the door.

Jakey took off his flat service cap and fitted his leather cane under one arm.

'Poppy! . . .' Jimmy murmured.

She marched to the door she had known earlier—found darkness.

'Where's our Little Man?'

Jimmy just stood there, dreaming her.

'Tim,' she said.

'Tim . . .' he echoed and scratched his head. 'Oh yes yes yes yes yes . . .' and he looked up the stairs as though hearing the boy suddenly up there.

He went first with the candle.

Suddenly he stopped and looked up at the sound of a distant explosion.

'Bejesus!' he whispered, 'will that be Jerry?'

'There's a raid,' Poppy said.

'There's not!' he said.

The sight of his room made Poppy's long act crack. She said, 'Very cosee!' dully.

'Mr. Lennox, where's Tim?' Jakey said firmly.

Jimmy took his time. Visions were like eggs. You couldn't lay the same one twice. You had to wait for another. 'They were there,' he said pointing to a particular floorboard and scratching his head. 'The two of them—and they said . . . now what was it they said to me . . . they said, Uncle Jim, we're going to . . . the *deep shelter* . . . *and when the raid's done we'll come back!*'

He cocked an eye at them to see how the tip would do. It was an old, disappointed eye, full of outsiders that came in last, pickled in blood and framed in encroaching creases, but it brightened, encouraged, at the spectacle of Poppy's extreme credulity. 'I can see them there,' he said with ineffable certainty, 'in warm safety!'

This time he used both hands to place them.

'Well, all we need do is wait,' Poppy said. Then to Jakey, 'You see, they're in the deep shelter.'

'Ai, that's right! You've said where they are! In the deep shelter!'

He stared at her, moved. She was like the best horse. A touch on her flanks and she'd have taken you to the moon. At that moment he shared, unknowing, the feeling for her of millionaires. She was better than gold. She was heaven. She made it bearable to be sober or absolutely rich. They must celebrate! Catch the moment! 'Poppy, me darlin',' he said in the agony of the effort, 'I was waitin' so long on you I just dropped off to sleep . . . But I said to meself if she comes back here with her charming gentleman and has to wait here for her children I'll give her just a bit of the sport she likes best in the world . . . Sit down, won't you?'

Poppy smiled, bewildered, and subsided rather fastidiously on to the edge of the one chair.

Jakey said, 'Can you tell me where this deep shelter is?'

'Well-I-could-now-I-could,' said Jimmy, turning from the shelf with a cardboard shoe-box. 'If there weren't just four of them, all about as close as the other. And each containing ten thousand souls with not enough air or light for a cat to find its heart's desire.'

'*Relax!*' Poppy said to Jakey. 'Take off your stays.'

Jakey made a helpless motion like a penguin balancing and sat on the edge of the bed, looking round.

Then he got up again. 'I think I'll try the billiard place.'

Jimmy said, 'That's right. They could be there.'

'I'll wait here,' Poppy said.

Jakey went out and found the café open. He pushed through the smelly blanket and came face to face with the pale man in the greasy white coat. All the little tables were empty, and the stairway was dark.

'Are those two young people here?' Jakey said.

The pale man said, 'They were back for a coat. Then they went away again.'

'A coat . . . ?'

'He'd lost his coat. The young boy like . . .'

Jakey had difficulty in pretending only mild interest. Ten years in the City helped.

'Thanks,' he said.

Back in Jimmy's room he saw a strange sight, Poppy and Jimmy sitting side by side on Jimmy's bed looking into the shoe-box.

'And that one there is Finnigan,' Jimmy said respectfully, 'he's got a great leg on him when he's in the mood!'

'Look, look,' Poppy crowed at Jakey. 'Your favourite things.'

Another set of bombs exploded, making the house jolt like a car going over a pothole.

Jakey had to peer and bend over low to focus seven large cockroaches standing in a state of expectation at the sudden breeze and dawn overhead. He loathed cockroaches.

'And I've a sort of a course,' Jimmy said modestly, producing a long cardboard channel, tacked together with pins. 'It's not just Aintree but won't it do for enthusiasts?'

He came into the light holding it and peering tentatively at their faces.

'What are we here for,' he said, placatingly, as though asking their pardon, 'on earth except to be as happy as we can . . . in the Circum-stances!'

Poppy agreed, laughing dottily.

'Well, then!' he said, seeking Jakey's permission with his eyes. 'How about a bit of a race on the flat . . . Colonel?'

'You look like a ghost!' Poppy confided to her lover. 'Cheer up . . . They're in a shelter, I told you.'

Jakey smiled thinly and put a modest sum on Finnigan. Then he sat down on Maureen's narrow bed, to watch.

27

A car like leaks of light from two keyholes, accompanied by a slow slushy sound of tyres, went by slow as a funeral walk.

'Oi,' Tim yelled, 'Taxi!' and held his hand up.

Then, cursing, he went after Maureen again but bumped into her, close.

'What's that then?' she said.

'I thought it might be a cab.'

'A cab . . .' she wondered, as though he had said camel. 'Don't yer want your jools then? . . . 'ere, 'ave a fruit-gum.

'Take another,' she said and tried to see his face. He might stick.

Her sister had gone away South, married. But so far it hadn't happened to her: the more boys she went with the less they stuck. Sometimes she felt as if she were being split in two, her body turned into a mere dirty, empty, smeared sardine tin quite separate from the part of her that prayed to the Virgin. So she sent her body away. In daydreams it got taken back—by Conrad; even sometimes when she was on the job with some man whose face she had never seen clearly and never would again. To-night she was all one, body and soul. She could imagine he would love her truly for ever, beneath waving palms. From the start his looks, unlike his speech, had needed no interpretation. Even now in the rosy dark Maureen's eyes made the journey which so many other, very different eyes—of both sexes—had made—in the flesh and by memory—before hers—along the full course of his face.

'You *want* your coat then?' She longed for him to want it badly and say so. But he, sensing this, wanted to take away from her even the right to mention it. So he said, 'What do you think? But I'm not going to traipse round Liverpool all night. Possibly the chances of recovery might be improved by daylight and a few constables.'

'Then you'd better go 'ome I mean 'adn't you,' she said missing the threat.

He began another taunt but the words died away in a helpless shrug.

'How?' he said roughly.

'I'll show you,' she said.

They went on.

Sometimes a lull would pave the way for the All-Clear. But the hope would pass when façades of buildings flickered and seconds later their ears were boxed by more explosions.

They were in a shopping street when suddenly the air became plaintive with the thin tune of a falling bomb. Maureen, experienced, threw herself down and Tim followed. The ground quaked while they lay in a big doorway.

Things fell tinkling. Afterwards Tim wanted to stay where he was and not move. He felt he didn't know enough about their destination to want to get there; or about any destination.

'C'm on then,' she said.

There was silence. He just lay, head down.

'Yer scared, aren't you . . . Hold my hand.'

He felt his hand taken. Her fingers squeezed his gently.

'It's cold on the ground,' she said. 'Can I 'ave a bit of your coat.'

She helped herself, opening it and putting the lower flap between her body and the pavement.

They lay there—for years it seemed. Like a crusader and his lady, petrified. The proximity in time hatched an event. She pulled his hand, and it, the hand, suddenly like an animal excluded from the feeding trough, barged in, free of hers and came to rest on her body. While he thought:

She's dirty, her dress wouldn't do for dusters. I'll catch something from touching her . . . like a parrot talking in an empty house.

His hand moved, discovered the curve of a hip bone and then the roundness of her thigh and farther away the secret firm softness of her bottom. Divine elasticity. With quickening blood he changed his position. Guns banged him back, then more furiously forward. He rose higher opposite her, and suddenly buried his lips into the side of her neck with a movement more suggestive of fighting, biting, disembowelling—all to get past dirt, *dirt:* and his hands were rough then gentle by turns; soon too eager like those of a looter fearing the return of some perpetual police. A hard spring of fattened but homeless flesh arrived between them, making imperious unspecified demand. He was on the verge of tears too, or of something . . . of some *feeling*, other than fear and negation.

'There,' she said softly, more like a breath than a word, 'there, Tim!' She murmured more often and herself became frantic: 'I don't mind with you, Tim . . . I don't mind you . . . Oh Tim, you're the one—the one I've wanted so long.' A long outpouring: soon merely a noise meaning: *come on.* One of her hands pulled him peremptorily, like the movement of a teacher in a dance that leaves no time for mistakes. Too late . . . she rolled about from side to side, began to toss and churn and suddenly he felt a hand, a frantic hand on him, hurting him. He found himself holding her down as though she were an antagonist, and this merely drove her to further frenzy, till suddenly she went limp as though a devil had been cast out. Then he had to do miserably what he'd often done alone while she lay beside him as though dead, her eyeballs gleaming in some stray light, but with her hand moving gently on his cheek.

Could he have been infected? The wish for such safety was obtained at some obscure but all too familiar cost. Isolation. He lay for a moment, feeling that this which he had so often coveted in imagination had again eluded him after coming close. A sense of nameless loss had increased.

'I love you, Tim,' she whispered. 'We'll go there together now, won't we?'

He listened to the madness of it. Tried to measure it.

He listened to it.

Then footsteps and a ring of light with a halo dazzled his eyes, and a rough, censorious voice asked who they were and what they were doing. Tim said he was on his way to the Alhambra Hotel.

'Well, you won't find it down there, son!'

The beam fell to Maureen's legs and thin shoes, wet from damp, then to Tim's clothing. Silence.

'C'mon then. That's enough,' said another voice.

A van slowed by the group. The voice of a woman who might have been in the drawing-room at Garston called, 'Are they all right? . . . He looks concussed.'

'Is that what you call it.'

'Can you take me to the Alhambra?' Tim said.

'Certainly,' said the woman.

' 'Op in,' said a man's voice. 'Always room for another.'

'What about you, dear?' said the woman.

The voice was vibrant as though the Germans had scattered love.

Maureen said she was going home.

'Where's that?'

'T'other way,' she said.

Tim climbed in, then looked back for Maureen but a torch was blinding him.

'What about your coat?' came Maureen's voice.
'No woonder the birth-rate's oop,' said the first voice.
The doors slammed.
Tim lay back against the metal.
And now something else was missing; bigger still.
He wanted to weep. The woman called over her shoulder:
'Bootle's bearing up magnificently.—Are you all right dear?'

28

The gleaming lozenge bodies of the cockroaches with their active fringes of legs made unequal progress along the cardboard straight. Sometimes they stopped or went backwards.

Poppy's attention wandered from such sport; her expression became morose and inturned. Boredom can achieve religious dimensions.

Jakey looked like a tailor's dummy abandoned in an attic, and Jimmy ill.

Poppy said to the 'favourite': 'Skidaddle!'

Jakey saw her go blind. He had seen the same look at Ascot, seen the hand loaded with rings go limp and the wonderful light go out of the eyes and be replaced by heaven knows what monster that posed, presumably, as her only friend; a dark adviser to whom she deferred whenever things went contrary.

'*I* think,' she suddenly declared, 'that Junior will have gone straight back to the hotel.' She looked for agreement at Jimmy. 'Do the buses run late?'

'You'll get one at one sometimes,' he said.

'You *see*,' she accused Jakey. 'She'll put him on a bus . . . or he'll get a cab. We can leave a message here and go back.'

She wanted to go back. And she was always an exhibitionist of what she wanted.

Her eyes rested on Jakey. '*What?*' she barked and looked sadder. He wondered how he could tell her that the coat was missing. Only by leaving this room. But what about Tim?

'I could stay here,' he said, 'and you could take the car and go back.'

'*Leave you here alone!*' She looked affronted.

'Tim was here all day alone.'

A look of amnesia made her face void.

She said, 'Tim . . . had his liddle friend.'

Jakey didn't know what to do. If she wanted to go, he couldn't stay. Equally, without Tim, he couldn't leave.

The cockroaches had fallen into a watchful inertia.

Jakey wondered how she would behave when she heard the coat had gone. He adjusted his spectacles with a neat octave-span touch of finger and thumb. Jimmy sighed like a fast puncture and said, 'That's about it.'

'Wurl . . .?' Poppy drawled, producing as she so often did, a mere ambiguous noise to take the place of several definite words. Jakey still didn't move.

Who can say if he would have given in? At that moment the sirens broke out, climbing slowly to the high level note of the All Clear. Poppy said, 'There you are!' as though somebody at least had had the good sense to heed her. And she stood up as though the official end of the raid restored Tim and his coat automatically to the hotel.

'There what?' Jakey said sternly, still sitting.

'He's in his bed.' She turned to Jimmy. 'Well, Jimmy, next time . . . Aintree!'

Jakey came unstuck then, overwhelmed by her spacious persuasions. He stood up.

'Good-bye,' Poppy began. Jimmy held up a hand, solemn as a pope.

'Good-bye my lady, then. God, it was a good experience seeing you! It was a kind of . . . a treat!'

She was uncertain about his meaning.

'Better luck next time,' she said, trying to recapture the

music of the duet which they had managed earlier. But she was out of tune, and Jimmy didn't join in. Not any more.

She went out hearing Jakey apologise for his aversion to cockroaches and thanking for shelter and 'your most courteous kindness.' On the stairs she thought *Bert's in the train* and wished Jakey would hurry.

The stars were shining. Fires gave rosy-linings to rooftops and chimneys. There were street voices, as after a party. She too for some obscure reason wanted to cry.

In the car Jakey told her the coat had gone. She didn't seem to understand at first.

'The coat's gone!'

When she believed it she sat in silence trying to digest it, visualising her husband, the next twelve hours . . . But it was too much for her.

Jakey was aware of an odd sound, a sort of soft vocal knocking beside him in the dark. 'Poppy,' he said and put out a hand thinking she was sobbing.

She was laughing, hopelessly, helplessly.

It was too much for Jakey. He started up and drove as though alone. 'Don't . . . *don't*,' she implored, 'I tell you: he's back in bed; the coat's over a chair. You see if it isn't!'

And of course she was wrong: Tim wasn't in their room. Jakey made a gesture in the doorway.

Duff's long fluffy tail, like a gorgeous ostrich feather flailed to and fro at the sight of his mistress. He came to the edge of the bed, as an admiral might to the edge of his ship, to see her piped aboard, and she for her part collapsed, lay back on the pillows which brought him galloping to her neck, where she gathered his snuffling face to hers impulsively as though all the heirlooms of Garston were less to her than the combings of his exquisite coat.

'Oosa brave boy!' she cried and wanted Jakey to admire the dog's courage.

Jakey put down his hat and stick and took off his spectacles to mop off the fog.

'Your dog,' he said, 'is safe.'

'It'll *turn up*,' she said.

'I seriously think we should ring the police.'

'He's fourteen.'

'You keep saying he's fourteen.'

'Well, he is. When I was fourteen I went to Antigua by myself.'

'And slept with your uncle when you got there.'

'That's what you think.'

'No. It's what you told me.'

'You're just scared of Bert,' she mocked.

It was so undeserved, so *vile*. Even Poppy recoiled from his face and from herself; lay back with Duff closing her eyes and said differently, 'O.K. The point is, *what can we do?* . . . Nothing. If you want to go back there, go. But I thought . . .'

'What?'

'You might like . . .'

He reprimanded her with his eyes.

They talked in circles; Poppy's voice became harsh and querulous, protesting her innocence, the inevitability. Jakey listing possibilities of action all of which she dismissed as irrelevant. Irrelevant to what? She fell silent. In the end he took the hint of her enormous and persistent omission, her increasing sadness, lying down beside her without his coat and glasses.

'Is that all you're going to take off?' she said.

'Could you put the dog away?'

The ceaseless bubbling of Duff's porous but congested nose receded as Poppy pushed him over and away.

She got up.

Jakey shut his eyes, listening to the sound of her undressing.

Perhaps at last! he thought, almost too tired to look forward even to his 'little treat.' Three a.m. last night; 2 a.m. to-night.

He massaged his eyes, touched his ribs, thought: afterwards back to Light Street to see if he could find Tim because even if search were futile, it would be at least search—Walking back to the bed Poppy stopped in her tracks : he was asleep. A look of surprise gave place to a smile, as though she had taken an unexpected trick at bridge. And she began tucking him up, methodically, taking off his shoes and in general putting him to rights. Then she covered him with an eiderdown. And that really was how she liked them: first as a foil, then dependent. She lay down beside him with Duff. After thinking a bit about Tim she too fell asleep with her hand on his. Duff lying in the fold of her knees, from which position the dog soon looked up petrified, because a sudden shaft of light from the passage split the room in two framing a tall silhouette. Terror strangled his growl to a mutter; Poppy stirred, turning her eyes from the light, spoke vaguely . . . the door closed. Jakey's head fell back again: soon he was again sitting in a fire-engine being driven by Bertrand. They were looking for Poppy. Bertrand knew where she was. But he didn't. They searched. Ringing a bell.

Outside in the passage, after that eyeful, Tim began walking back, tapping the wall bleakly every few steps with the back of his knuckles.

'They did it,' he thought.

The biggest sofa downstairs was in the lounge with the glass doors in the smell of stale smoke. He made for it. Years ago he had been at Eton and answered Absence. Yet now, already it was then, far, far ahead, and far away, as he blundered down the stairs.

The night-watchman at the desk, Mr. Fred Letter, raised his face. To Tim the features gleamed, faint as a luminous watch under bedclothes, above the evening paper. Mr. Letter was surprised. But his interest was not even faintly returned; the boy was already dreaming, and waiting only for the musty velveteen cushions to regularise his condition.

He slumped down and the side of the chair brought to his notice a strange lump in his pocket.

He put in his hand and took out a coloured ball about the size of a ping-pong ball, rather grubby and faintly sticky. Then he remembered! The amusement arcade, the soupy loudspeaker and the woman with the ill face, promising him a prize. Surely not yesterday!

An immense depression came over him, such as he got during house-parties at Garston; when his father shouted, slewed round from the bridge table shouting . . . Then he would take refuge in a room covered with dust-sheets, propping his book in a mortuary of furniture and ancestors, breathing a smell of cold polish and desertion taking comfort from facts about dinosaurs and his own dogma of 'racial senescence.'

Now he wished for it all, even the ballroom at Christmas, even his father losing at bridge, yelling . . . 'two diamonds.'

29

Maureen was used to being left on a pavement without a word. So the quick disappearance of Tim was almost expected like the torch beam and the man's voice telling her to go home and keep off the streets.

She loitered away from the wardens and then stood in doubt as to where she should go next. Half of her was sure she would never see Tim again, the other half said Conrad came back for Lana after she had saved him from the octopus. The second half prevailed. Her mother had given her everything, even the thing she needed most herself, food. And somehow the rhythm of that behaviour carried on inside the girl so that she was immune to resentment. Her infant brother had screamed, Jimmy had bullied and now a boy asked for something and offered nothing. She gave what they needed. It was her role. Her power and identity.

She continued along the street, the way she had been going, daftly resolute, pulling her coat tighter at the throat against the night wind. Somehow people became more real for her when they weren't there. Tim joined her mother; became divine. An ideal, like Conrad.

She dreamed, asleep almost on her legs as she entered the darkened court behind the Rialto cinema where Lou lived with his wife, her mother's cousin.

No light showed anywhere. Maureen knew most people wouldn't have called at this house even in day, certainly not her aunt or uncle. But she went up the few stone steps and banged confidently. To have tapped, after a night of explosions would have seemed silly. And soon she banged again all the louder because of the fear she began to feel.

Suddenly she heard the muffled harshness of a man's voice. And footsteps. Then her cousin stood there in a dressing-gown clutched to her, hair anyhow, and eyes staring like a frightened cat, ready to hiss . . . which she did.

'Who's that then? . . . *Maureen!*'

'It's for me broother's coat. Lou took it off the peg like at the billiards. By mistake.'

'. . . Yer brother?'

'Colin's home.'

'*Colin!*'

Such an event was too much to believe.

And the woman didn't try.

But she said, 'Maureen . . . ! It's past two!'

After a moment Tilly said lower still:

'Lou 'ad an extra coat,' and she looked uncertainly over her shoulder. 'It's yours, is it?' she said.

'Sort of blue like. 'Airy,' Maureen said.

'I said to 'im: "it don't fit you." ' Tilly sounded virtuous, indignant.

'. . . Well, then,' Maureen murmured.

'But 'e said to get it altered for 'im, see? 'E said it was good stuff. Thick.'

'It's ours,' Maureen said.

Tilly's face hardened, became outcast.

Maureen said nothing. She stooped a little inside her coat, using her arms as protection for her ribs against the night air. Tilly's eyes dropped down the figure of her young relation, ending at the shoes.

'Wait there,' she snapped. A moment later she stuffed the coat roughly into Maureen's hands. 'Get on home then . . .

Kind of heavy, innit? How's Jimmy? . . . That's right. Say I was asking for him. Go on then, Maureen. Terrible night, wasn't it . . . Any down your way . . . Looked like it, ta-ta then, Maureen.'

No one ever crossed Lou's smallest wish. No one. So Maureen stood there an extra second. A ceremonial pause!

Tilly said, 'That's it, then. Won't make much odds . . .'

'Ta.'

Then the door closed and Lou's voice could be heard complaining, cajoling.

Maureen raced away. She was flying, flying to Conrad, to Tropic Palms. She could see his face. Kissing. Good-bye Jimmy, she said, Good-bye.

The glow of burning warehouses helped her dream with an illusion of tropical sunset. She loved a sunset, a real gory one, with a golden passage all the way to the sun. On the last page.

30

Poring over the shrunk back columns of the Liverpool *Evening News* where football had turned into a mockery of its former self, Fred Letter licked a finger and having turned back to the middle where there was a heading 'COAL FOR ALL' and a picture of Lord Bewick and another of Dorothy Lamour pushing out her bosom for N.A.A.F.I. and sucking in her waist, till her head looked like something stuck on. He coughed. Though passed-over for head porter in 1937, he was a Sidesman at St. Peter's, Lutheran. Raising his left hand, Mr. Letter placed it in the position which would have been occupied by a beard had he had one, spanning from cheekbone to cheekbone, thumb one side fingers the other and palm under his chin, slowly pulling the whole hand downwards as though he were indeed stroking. Then he tilted his head a little backward so as to see the woman sometimes blurred through the top and sometimes clear through the bottom of his bifocals, thus giving the picture the benefit of variety and even obscurity.

At last he made a turgid noise, '*Charr* . . .' And then having licked his finger again and returned to the ghost of football he suddenly said, 'She's all yours, mate!' and began coughing, an episode which he brought to fruition with an open-mouthed *Yarrr tch* noise, and expectoration, into a red handkerchief.

By which time there were five minutes less of the night,

a fact he checked, pedantically, through the top of his spectacles cocking his forehead forward like a goat about to charge.

Then he raised his right index finger to his tongue till he had summoned up some spittle, took hold of the dog-ear, loosened the page from its mate with a little flipping ritual . . . and turned back to the Bit of Vain Dorothy La Bustle, smiling parsimoniously at the name he had given her and the idea of the smack, which was about all he/she was good for, when it came to the said vain bustle.

At that moment he heard a sound and his chin came down at once to facilitate vision. He got sailors in here after a raid: one'd been sick in the ferns last Tuesday and it wasn't happening again.

'Ay!' he reprimanded though without, yet, a target.

'I can see yer!' he lied.

Perhaps it was only the boy who had gone into the lounge going back. So he looked through the glass doors. But the boy was still there, sprawled upright in an arm-chair, head angled and hands dug deep into his pockets, in the exact position from which Mr. Letter had tried to rouse him, an hour ago, without success.

So he turned back to where he thought he'd already looked, near the swing door. Suddenly, much closer, a pale face emerged and to his relief developed a grey body. It was a girl, a proper little slut, Mr. Letter thought, one of them Irish or he was a Dutchman.

'And what do *you* want?' he said.

Maureen did not like the look of Mr. Letter.

She was chewing gum. And Mr. Letter wondered what she did to get it. He began to look rather like a magistrate on the bench. You could tell she was Under Age. Soon she'd be Under Arrest.

'Ay?' he commanded. 'What's all this?'

''Ave you got Tim Loxley staying 'ere?' she said.

'What's that got to do with you?' he said.

''E left 'is coat.'

Mr. Letter looked at the coat which she held up. It was the only thing that made sense being clean enough to examine. He found the name-tape: *T. Loxley.*

'What d'you expect me to do with it?'

'Give it 'im.'

Mr. Letter was offended by her simplicity.

'Give it to 'oo? 'Ow do I know we've a Mr. Loxley. Look . . .' he said and he waved a hand at the long ranks of vacant hooks. 'Reception's off.'

Maureen pushed out her lips, and put her hair back, waiting for something better to happen. Mr. Letter was scandalised. It was obvious she might do anything. Here, in the foyer. Supposing someone came. He rose and took off his spectacles so that he had the comfort of putting them on again a moment later when he had crossed the hall. There he switched on a light above the register, fussed with the pages, and complained about increasing responsibility without commensurate increase in pay, about Irish waifs in a city already short of facilities and rich in unwanted babies, about people who left coats in places he didn't care to imagine and Miss Jock whose handwriting in the ledger proved beyond doubt that in fifty years we had moved fast backwards from the modest goal of the three Rs.

'Scollop,' he said suddenly as though she could take that and be grateful.

'Well?' he said, quizzing over the top. 'Scollop?'

'Tim Loxley,' she said. 'Like in the coat.'

Should he accept such impudence? In a way it was a help, chipping the night away nicely.

He sniffed and raised an index finger to his tongue; but it had already given too much in the way of saliva. For more he had to do something with his cheeks and jaws, working up wetness. The effort brought on a cough, which he got down to. A minute or two later when he had brought it to juicy fruition and stowed away the yield in his red handkerchief, wrapped on this occasion for Maureen's benefit in three directions and tucked high like a buttonhole, he looked painfully put upon.

Suddenly he looked sad: 'Lady Bewick . . . Loxley,' he admitted, and held out his hand for the coat. ''Oo shall I say brought it?'

Maureen was looking round, eyes fixed on the glass doors of the lounge.

Fred Letter was not surprised she preferred to remain anonymous. He gave her another look over the top: six months without the option.

'You'd better get along,' he said.

'That's 'im there,' she said, still staring.

Mr. Letter had had enough. He arranged a pencil alongside a pen swiftly asserting order and the invisible cash price of favours in this place. In which respect she compared unfavourably with the sailor who had been sick in the ferns.

'Look,' he said. 'You aren't by any chance stayin' at this hotel, are you? . . . Well, then, the door's over there!'

'Can I speak to 'im?' she said.

''Asn't 'e paid you?' said Mr. Letter unpleasantly.

Maureen flushed. Her eyes shone. She said, 'You nickety Old Goat.' And she dropped the coat on the floor.

''Ere!' he pointed a stiff finger at her with passion. This was the very place where one of the pages said the very same the day after he should have become head porter in '36. He began to shudder. And she began to drift away.

'That's better,' he said. 'Go back where you belong.'

He couldn't tell her to shut the door, it being a swing-door, but he made a kind of a noise suggestive of rubbish-disposal.

Maureen stopped and looked again so hard at the sleeping

boy that Mr. Letter was driven out of the rut of his hostility and turned, following her eyes, questioning in his turn the object of her interest as though she had the power to change whatever she looked at.

Perhaps half a minute passed. And he let it, not knowing why.

'Now then!' he said turning back to her. 'We don't want the coppers in 'ere, do we?' and he put his hand on the telephone.

She drifted out and away. The brushing sound of the swing-door continued for a moment after she had vanished.

A moment later Mr. Letter was bewildered . . . *frightened.*

Had *anyone* been in?

He looked rather sharply down at the coat, stooped, picked it up, put it aside and then returned to his newspaper as though he hadn't ever left it. But a moment later he looked again in the direction of the swing doors, and then at the place where she had stood . . . then at the boy . . .

He was rescued by a tickle. The coughing took him to 1.40 by the stairs clock.

Tim stirred in his sleep, as Mr. Letter, again moistened, with difficulty, his index finger and turned back from Vain Bustle and 'COAL FOR ALL' to the shrunk reports of almost anonymous teams, containing here and there hidden crumbs of nourishment: Stan Matthews a flipping sergeant . . .

Another noise. Fast, light footsteps. Mr. Letter prepared to butt again, peering . . .

This time an officer in gig-lamps strode down the stairs, raised a leather cane in salute and vanished into the swing-doors.

Proper night of it, Mr. Letter thought. Blitz, ghosts and fornication. The lot! All for three quid a week.

*Yarr*ICH!—and he was off again.

31

Jakey never got back into 42 Light Street. The door seemed to have gone solid, the house dead. He was not really surprised. Poppy's capacity for making things happen sometimes struck him as a branch of witchcraft and without her he had not much hope of finding Irish waifs in sickly slums. In fact he was slightly surprised to have even found the house—as though it and all that had happened in it had been the machination of his exhausting witch.

It's true of course that he did not like to hammer too hard on the door. People, he thought, must be sleeping everywhere after such a night, and if Tim had been there he would have been waiting up, surely . . .

So just when dawn was beginning to break over the dying fires, Jakey reached the telephone outside his hostel bedroom and rang the Alhambra, interrupting a man in mid-cough, and asking for Lady Bewick.

'She's asleep,' Letter claimed. Jakey did not deny it, and certainly she must have been judging by her 'Hallo'.

After some accusing noises, almost words, she did manage the ghost of concern, saying: 'He wasn't there! . . .' then, 'Goch . . .' liquefying the last consonant of the deity in an escape of unhappy breath.

He said he had told the police.

She became more awake, immediately questioning the

rightness of such action, then subsiding when he explained: he hadn't mentioned the coat.

There was then a silence.

'Well, there you are——' she tailed off.

'What d'you mean?'

'It would have been far better to wait till morning. It's *obvious* where he is. Where I said all along—with that dopey little tart.'

'That child?'

'Child!'

'. . . Tim?' Jakey said. 'With her?'

'Oh, don't be such an idiot,' she said. 'If I were yooo I'd seize a little shut-eye, before Uncle Bertie hits Liverpool. Soon we're all going to be busy!'

'Poppy, I've done all I can. I'm going back to London after breakfast.'

Then she did wake up. He certainly had *not* done all he could. She wanted him to-morrow more than ever before, 'with Bert raving round.' Did he love her at all?

Jakey standing painfully in his Sam Browne, in a draught, holding one side, felt slowly stupider and happier as he listened to her voice vibrant with tears, indignation and suffering. Her need created him. He closed his eyes as he listened.

'Besides . . .' she said. 'There's a Reward for you. Don't you want it?'

'Poppy, *je t'adore!*'

There was silence. Then she said very low, almost unrecognisable, '*Do* you? Because if *you* don't . . .'

'Finish your sentences,' he said—and smiled because he could finish the lie for her. And he was touched to the heart, made to feel strong by this tiny juggernaut in bracelets, Bertrand's moll—who was really so weak, weaker, more prone to feelings of non-entity even than himself. That was why she showed off all the time. He made another kissing sound into the mouthpiece as though to a child and heard it come back, *meekly*.

'Whatever, wherever, whenever,' he said.

'That's a bit better!' she whispered through her tears—a wispy echo of an exhausted burglar getting a safe open.

32

Tim heard his father's voice but there was nothing to confirm it. The heavy brown furniture, the old copy of *The Motor*, the ash-trays, the stale smell were all part of yesterday in which his father had no possible place.

Sleep nipped the corners of his eyes. He sat up.

And *saw* his father: shouting at the porter, a man with pince-nez. Electric light was still burning.

'Then I advise you to *make* it your business.'

Tim had heard his father scream before. When it was like this in public he usually went away. But there was nowhere to go. Besides, here it was different. Yesterday lay behind like a pit. A void. The shaping strokes of his father's will-power had been missing. It was almost a satisfaction to hear them now. Losing the coat in some curious way seemed to have restored to him his father.

Losing the coat had brought his father! That was what it felt like.

Tim sat there apathetically, at home.

For Fred Letter the experience was also familiar. Here in the very desk that might have been his by day, in peace time, instead of half his by night in war-time, he had at last snatched a sickly doze from the ruins of the night. The little life left in him had been a mere trickle when suddenly a man as big as the late head porter threatened to get him sacked even from nightshift during war.

Mr. Letter was conscious as never before of a Pattern. He could not *go on* coming out worst in this place. Soon there wouldn't be any more opportunities for a difference. So when Lord Bewick shouted '*Now move!*'—like an R.S.M.—but without the prerogative, Mr. Letter drew his whole life story up to its full height, said quietly, 'I will!' and sat down, licking as he did so with deliberation the index finger of his right hand and separating, with a ritualistic flip, the top page from the bottom of the Liverpool *Evening News*.

Tim heard a curious trombone note from his father's gullet. In the beginning was the Word—the word of *Pithecanthropus Erectus*.

Mr. Letter looked up sharply over his bifocals and said, 'What was that?'

At this moment appeared Miss Jock of Reception, but she too, like a tourist caught in a riot, was soon swept into the orbit of violence.

Being young and impressionable she was frightened. Her keys froze. She just managed to keep her head. Training can be a help sometimes.

'Lady Bewick is in 207,' she said. 'If you'd care to leave your case, sir, I'll have it sent up.'

'Whassat coat doing there?' Lord Bewick suddenly snapped pointing at the garment lying at Letter's elbow. Fred looked at it with as much surprise as any. He had forgotten it.

And Tim seeing it thought: *She found it.*

Mr. Letter said, 'A street woman brought that in. It's for a Mr. Loxley.'

Lord Bewick's voice went husky. 'Give it to me!'

'I can't do that!' Letter said.

Miss Jock was frightened for her frail colleague and moved towards the garment, thus saving Bertrand the last foot or so of a snatch. He shook it open and turned it this way and that. 'Fetch me a tailor,' he whispered.

Letter stood up. 'I'll 'ave that coat back now, please!' and he held out a hand.

Bertrand turned towards the lifts.

Letter whipped after him. Whatever happened, happened round the corner: Tim heard terrible shouting: and he could see the face of the girl behind Reception. That was enough. Then Letter came back ashen talking to himself, folding up his newspaper, arranging pen and pencils, getting his coat, talking to the girl, coughing, coughing, worse than ever, buttoning up the old raincoat while the sound of the lift sang in the walls.

Tim stared numbly at the swing-doors. 'Cur-eist,' he said scratching his head and shaking it as though to get cobwebs out. He began to feel invisible, grey, like that vast window of sea. The old apathy engulfed him. The arrival of his father confirmed it. He toyed with the idea of going out somewhere to breakfast, and of staying out for quite a time. Yes, all day, and to-morrow. He wouldn't mind disappearing altogether. But he was hungry. As he trudged past Miss Jock, she said into the receiver, 'He's just here Lady Bewick,' and then to him, 'Mr. Loxley, please.'

He hung back a moment.

Poppy's voice was jumpy, staccato, claiming him. 'TIM?'

'Well,' he said.

'TIM!'

The second explosive, grabbing cry made him boil with contradictory emotions. She exulted and lectured him.

He heard her exult to his father.

'Come up!' she crowed. 'We've got a little coat of yours! All complete!'

'If you don't mind *awfully* I'll have breakfast down here,' he said.

'But your Pop's here,' she protested.

'I rather gathered as much actually.'

'Why didn't you sleep in your *bed*, you nut!'

'It was already occupied,' he said.

Then suddenly there was his father's voice luscious with satisfaction.

'Tim . . . Good boy. Where d'you sleep? . . . on the tiles, eh?'

'In a chair.'

His father seemed satisfied by this too.

'Leaving your life-jacket around?'

'Merely with trusted retainers . . .'

'Silly boy. See you then, after breakfast.' The receiver came down even as Tim replied, 'Yupp.'

Then Tim went to the Residents' dining-room.

Passing the same big window he loitered a bit in front of the vast expanse of sea, now bright with early sun and spotted with ships and boats of all sizes. The waitresses were looking at him. Only then did he remember he was still wearing his great-coat—and no jacket.

'Would you think it awfully odd if I ate my breakfast in this get up?' he said. 'The truth is I passed a somewhat unusual night.'

He could do no wrong with the waitresses. Two were pleased to stand near while he frowned at the menu.

One of his elbows was sore where he must have lain on something hard. He raised it to see if there was a hole in the coat. But it was merely dirty.

His thoughts drifted violently . . .

He scratched his head and said roughly, 'Kipper' and then fixed his eyes on the sea, narrowing them against the great brightness of sunlit water.

33

Dawn that day came as usual to No. 42 Light Street, stealing through the threadbare curtains, showing up slowly the patch of damp like a map of India above the fireplace and throwing into relief the humped forms of Jimmy Lennox and his niece. The cockroach racecourse lay where last used and the whisky bottle still on its side where first empty. Jimmy's clothes were on him and Maureen's sprawled on a chair except the grey coat, with the fur trimming (that always looked wet), which was spread over her body. In time Jimmy groaned and lit a fragment of cigarette which he smoked at risk to his fingers, staring up at the ceiling as though demanding from it a single reason for getting up.

At one point the presence of Maureen—which he checked on with some difficulty since it meant moving his head and neck beyond the angle that was easy, gave him food for thought, though not a square meal. He took a last puff which meant swallowing fire like a damned circus performer. He threw the ashes away with pain in his fingers and disgust in his mouth. Had she got some money for to-day? God, he thought (and his mind started to whirr like a piece of released clockwork), there was this boy beautiful as an angel and he said to my daughter Maureen, I'll not take what you might think fit to offer because I can see as plain as the statue of Monsignor Nugent in St. John's Gardens that beneath your trim overcoat and split shoes you're the true royal Lennox in a damned dirty hole of a country far from home, bombed by Germans and inspected by the Witches Voluntary Service after the police themselves have turned you into a striptease nightly with the spot of their idle torches: so instead I'll give you what is exactly the equivalent of a whole fiver to my father, I'll give you ten thousand gold pounds, which I brought along with me specially on account of all I'd heard of your famous uncle and foster-father Jimmy Lennox, since merely to see the man is to receive something priceless. To which she answers: 'Tim, it's your wisdom that surprises me!' And he: 'It's not wisdom . . . it's plain as a poke in the eye!'

At this moment Maureen stretched and sat up.

'Well?' Jimmy said.

She said nothing.

'Did you have a great night perhaps the two of you . . . ?'

She pulled her coat up round her and went to the gas ring flicking it on tentatively and listening for the *huff*. He could see the shape of her: a fortune on two legs.

'What did you get then?' he said.

Maureen lit the gas and went out into the passage with her clothes. He had tried something once, in the morning. It was the dressing that started him. So she came back dressed and said, 'I got what I wanted, see.'

His heart leapt like a lamb in country.

'That's right,' he approved.

He liked her tough. It made him feel safe.

She got a loaf out and a tin of tea, a jar of jam. In the end he couldn't bear the doubt.

'But how much?'

'Nothing.'

She was a great one for a tease, but overdid it.

'I'm telling you,' she said.

'You're joking, Maureen.' His wounded eyes followed the roughness of her movements.

'Come on,' he said, beginning to threaten.

He nagged her round the room demanding an explanation.

'I put the roof over your head and the clothes on your body and then you say "nothing"! . . . What were you doing then?'

'Fetching 'is coat.'

'What coat?'

'He left 'is coat in the billiards and Lou took it.'

Jimmy didn't hear the name; it had gone from memory even while being mentioned.

'So you went with him?'

'We got 'is back. I did. Tilly gave it me.'

'With her husband's permission?'

Maureen didn't answer.

'You went there,' Jimmy said weakly. He looked away from her, closed his eyes, and his hand subsided on his chest like a tired bishop, prostrate. 'Mother of God,' he murmured. 'Why didn't you get another coat—you could have had mine. My last.'

''Cos 'is was full of diamonds.'

She gave him then the first look of the morning, couldn't resist it. She had to laugh.

'What's that?' he whispered.

'Your face,' she said.

She crunched into a bit of toast, put the toast down and shook her hair back ready for the brush.

'God alive,' he muttered. 'Diamonds . . . and you . . .' Then with relief he saw she was at it again. Joking.

Something maddened her and she said: 'They was in parcels sewn up into the lining. You could feel them like sweets.'

He was bewildered.

'Where are you going?'

She had risen and seized her coat.

'Wherever you aren't,' she said. In the passage she started

to cry. *Oh holy Mother!* She saw the shadowy Virgin of St. Patrick's with her hands open like the kind nun at Hedgely. And so she prayed, upright: I could go with him over the sea to America, I would love him, and I'd never sin again, never, never. If You'll let him take me with him, away from here.

The conditions seemed so reasonable that she stopped there.

And Jimmy called out 'Poisoner!'

He meant it too! Diamonds! it was the kind of thing women said to spite the hope that a man carried about in his heart. They were all the same, all poisoners. Spiteful. Just to deprive him she had let slip a great opportunity. Diamonds or not the boy must have had money to burn. Better if he had never come! On every other night when there had been a raid she had taken better money than usual. Last night should have been a record. And what did she get? Nothing. And who gave her shelter?

His face corrugated with the tightening pain of his conviction that the child was against him. Why? Because she was female. What did a man usually get from women!

A desire to be revenged on her grew in him as he lay on the bed wondering at his deprivation. But direct expression of anger would not have been safe. There was always to-morrow, always his need of her. So he sensed a way of hurting her which far from driving her away would keep her closer. He said: 'So you took that man's coat! While he was sleeping.'

He heard her outside, knew she was listening.

'Begod, Maureen, you'd better work hard, hadn't you? That man's new coat! How will you pay it back? . . . Or will you just wait *till he pays you back*?'

He went on and on and she heard it all. And she imagined the rest. Lou! The name people never uttered. Once in a café she had seen a girl whose whole face was red like a rag that had been partly dipped in red paint. There had been a sort of mouth with white lips beside the real mouth with red lips and blood everywhere, even on the table and she remembered the high whimpering noise that came out of the real mouth. Jimmy kept on at her.

She had never known anything like this moment, this empty morning . . . She looked down the stairs. *I'd like to die, she thought, to-day . . .*

Although she'd finished dressing, she didn't go back in, she just leant against the wall feeling the tears drying on her cheeks. Listening to the sound of him—and weighing him against her aunt, Mrs. Oliphant and Chester.

'I've got a quid,' she shouted suddenly.

He stopped.

But she still didn't go in. She closed her eyes and wondered. Two new petitions in the Lady Chapel would work. Holy Mother . . . she began and with every word Tim-Conrad—came nearer.

She had done her part, hadn't she? Done what she'd been told. She had been good. . . .

34

Tim went up in the end. But he kicked the door the last inches.

'She was only a Horse Trainer's daughter!' his father said showing the gold tooth, grinning the proud suggestion. His relief filled the room; and his Turkish tobacco smoke.

'Wuh?' he said. 'Where is she?'

Poppy was stitching a long vent in the coat, where Bertrand had just performed a violent Cæsarian with her nail-scissors. She didn't look up.

'What on earth . . . ?' Tim said.

'Nice liddle girl, was she?' his father pursued and gripped Tim's shoulder. 'Let's hear about it.'

Poppy did not want her husband to hear a word about it. She had avoided a row only by underlining the respectability of the "trainer"—and his daughter.

Tim said: 'What I'm interested in is how much longer I'm going to be stuck here with you, Poppy and A. N. Other.'

They were used to him of course. But Poppy minded, this time. She gave him a level gangster's look and bit off the thread.

'Well?' said Tim.

'You're off this afternoon,' his father said. 'They've just rung through.'

'Well, thank *God*,' Tim said.

'He can't wait to get among all those priddy girls and

popcorn,' Bert said, still holding his son's shoulder, pushing it a bit. Like Jimmy.

Tim freed himself fastidiously.

'What's it like in Light Street?' his father said. 'You went to a movie with your little friend? Was that where you left your coat behind . . . ?' His grin was warm, proud, almost salacious. He wanted to hear everything.

'She must have brought it back,' Tim said to Poppy.

Poppy's fear of her husband knowing the facts yielded to curiosity. 'Don't you *know*?' she said.

Tim said, 'Well, who else could have brought it?'

'You were lucky,' Bert said gruffly.

Tim looked from one to the other, sensing something.

Poppy said dreamily, 'How about a little *quid pro quo* for Jimmy?' And at once regretted it.

Bert said, 'A box of cigars you mean?'

Poppy tried to conceal her tracks: 'He'd be insulted.'

She was bewildered by what she might have set in train.

'Then we can just thank them,' Bertrand said—his heart was full. So full that he began to walk.

'Yeah,' Poppy said. 'Write.'

Tim found so many lines crossed inside his own and apparently their heads also, that he scratched his hair and flung about and looked out of the window as though the only hope was what in fact was about to take place: emigration.

'How do we get there?' Bert said. 'Light Street.'

'We don't,' Poppy said. 'It's miles.'

'We've got time,' Bert said.

She plied her needle.

'What's Jakey doing?' Bert said.

'He's maybe gone,' she said.

'He hasn't,' Tim said. 'He rang me when I was downstairs. He says he's telling the police that I'm found.'

'*The police* . . .' Lord Bewick said.

'We told them a boy had gone; not a coat,' Poppy said quickly.

Tim looked at his father, who paced a bit.

'I want to thank Jakey too,' Bert said suddenly radiating thanks. 'He could help us kill two birds with one stone. Visit Tim's friends and then go on to the ship.' He had begun to breathe like a puffed horse, with the momentum of his gratitude. Tim moved his knees clear to give his father room to work it off.

Poppy looked morose, stitching.

'Now you're going to ask him to drive *you*!' she objected.

Her mouth flickered.

'Why not!' and Bert walked over to the telephone and a moment later rapped out the name of the Officers' Club, smiling, smiling specially.

She thought: *Wherever*, *whenever*, *whatever*.

'Jakey!' And then, in a few words, it was arranged. Jakey would take them to the ship.

Bert grinned, or was it a sort of scowl.

Poppy stitched.

'Well-a-well,' she said. 'Whaddyaknow!'

Tim swung his penknife in circles, first one way, then the other.

Bert paced a bit more and picked the side of one nostril with his thumbnail. 'Good!' he said as though remembering their presence. 'That's settled.'

'Well, I think you're craz-ee,' Poppy murmured, 'to go all the way out there . . . for nothing. Send them something.'

'No. Tim ought to go in person,' Bertrand said. 'Even if it's only to thank them.'

Poppy's eyes narrowed upwards in sardonic refocusing of the rent coat.

35

Later. The sky had cleared and the cobbles shone in the wet.

Jakey drove. Beside him Tim, and in the back side by side, Bertrand and Poppy. The experience reminded Jakey of his dream, though in that instance Bert had been the driver and the vehicle a fire engine. Poppy the quarry. But what is the difference, sometimes, between dream and reality? At times reality can hold its own.

'What a piece of luck,' Bertrand said with bubbles in his voice, 'that Jakey was up here on duty,' and he smiled forgiveness at the driving mirror, showing his brilliant dog-tooth and looked down at Poppy and putting one big hand on her thigh, while she looked away through the window, like a punished child.

Jakey said, 'At least it's calm. You won't be seasick.'

Tim was trying to recognise the streets, and to believe in yesterday, or to-morrow.

'I don't know *why* we have tc go back there,' Poppy said.

Bertrand imagined a villa surrounded by white palings with prints of Stubbs's horses above the fireplace, framed originals of Newmarket transactions for famous horses in the eighteenth century, presentation silver cigarette boxes, from associations. He waited for a turning off into suburbs.

Soon he said, 'Have you lost your way?'

It was then that Jakey guessed what had happened.

They slowed at a corner. Three lascars in ill-fitting suits and sandals looked in at them.

'Lucky your little popsy didn't know what you had in your pocket,' Bertrand said, half to himself, and he looked out on the grey streets, still feeling that things had fallen into place as usual. He wheezed a little as he breathed, holding on to the silken support at one side of the window. He began smiling as though to rinse everybody's ears and nerves of the other sounds to which he had recently subjected them. His hand remained on Poppy's thigh and his smile transferred itself to the back of his son's motionless head, and became soft, complacent and sentimental, picturing the success of his young rogue with the daughter of the racehorse trainer. Then his eyes rested on the material of the special coat while he congratulated himself on having the job properly done by the proper people, without which one of the stable-boys would certainly have noticed something odd, borrowed it and given the thing back only when he had modified it by about fifty per cent.

Tim said, 'She did know. I told her.'

'Knew what?'

'What was in the coat.'

Poppy couldn't face it. She said, 'Believe you me, she thought you were kidding.'

'Have you an *earthly* what you're talking about?' Tim burst out, 'Because if you haven't I'd put a sock in it.'

He turned round and stared at his stepmother with an expression that made her go back to looking sideways at the street.

'Were you *there* by any chance?' Tim pursued her bitterly.

'No,' she said.

'Well, then—kindly take a pace to the rear.'

She raised her eyebrows as though straightening away a tear. Everyone had taken leave of their senses. And why *against her* all the time? What had *she* done? Nothing.

'We just hoped you had a little more sense than to tell her,' she whispered.

The whipped look in her eyes changed into an expression that was haggard and contemptuous of everything under the sun. Her fingers sank into Duff's coat and worked there.

'She was an honest girl then,' Bertrand said with approval. 'You told her you had a few gold sovereigns in it.' He understood.

'*I told her:* I said I want my coat back *because it's full of diamonds.*'

Silence fell. Bertrand thought, Are the stones I've just seen *substitute fakes*? At last he said thickly. 'Why didn't you go and fetch it yourself?'

'Because it so happens that the man who took it was the biggest cut-throat in Liverpool. Lou Cochrane. A murderer if you really want to know.'

Something about his tone earned their uneasy attention.

'You mean you saw the man who took it?' his father said·

'He was playing billiards. He left his coat and took mine.'

'But you got it back. O.K.! For heaven's sake!' Poppy said. She raised her eyebrows again, made a face and then suddenly began laughing tearfully like an engine that has begun firing of its own accord, turning her face as far as possible from Bertrand who moved his hand from her thigh and said 'ungh': a sort of *cri de ventre*, at the streets they were going through.

He looked glazed. 'Where are we?' he said.

'Very nearly there,' Jakey said.

Poppy looked helplessly at the grey leprous façades of the Liverpool slums, the sodden rubbish in gutters, at the Victorian fixture demonstrating charity, a drinking well with a rusty lion-face and behind, above the verdigris bulbous dome of an institution. Then filthy dereliction of scrap yards and a smoky frieze of derricks and grey or camouflaged funnels.

Bertrand said vacantly: 'You came here yesterday . . . ?'

'I told you *he was bombed out*,' Poppy pleaded.

His silence encouraged her. When you have nothing to lose: attack. She took on her querulous governess tone.

'You live at Garston. You haven't a clue. If you're bombed out you're lucky to get a roof anywhere, no matter who you are.'

'Number 42,' Jakey said mildly. They had arrived.

Bertrand muttered—and took out a fiver, stretched over to Tim, 'Here, go and give her this.' He looked like a stranger.

'Why don't *you* give it to her?' Tim said violently, holding the money out, back.

'I wasn't the lucky guy,' his father said quietly. Poppy shrank, feeling the rage all round her.

Tim dropped the money on Poppy's lap. 'Then you can.'

'Look. D'you want your little friend to get it,' Poppy said curtly, 'or not?' and she gave it to him.

He snatched it and blundered out and up to the door where he used the knocker three times with violence. Jakey got out.

'We haven't got all that time,' Poppy called.

'Don't you want to see your Jimmy?' Tim mocked.

Jakey distracted him, taking him to the door again.

It opened and Maureen appeared. Jakey saluted. Bertrand grunted and leaned forward to see better. A heavy succulent smile spread over his face at the sight of the young face and figure. 'Quite a priddy girl,' he muttered. And soon it would be all over.

He wound down the window.

'Tim,' he called.

Tim's arm fell back in despair from the movement it had already begun without conviction.

'Give her a liddle kiss—and then another one from me.'

Poppy muttered, 'God!'

Bertrand shouted: 'Go *on*, man!'

Maureen stood there looking at them all as though she had never seen any of them before, not even Tim, or his coat.

Tim said: 'Hallo. By the way thanks awfully for getting the coat back. My father happens to have offered a reward. Here it is,' and he stuffed the money out.

Maureen's hand remained slack.

Tim felt he couldn't stand many more seconds in that place. He looked back at the car.

'Give her a kiss,' Bertrand repeated.

Suddenly Jimmy appeared at Maureen's shoulder. 'Look at that,' he said following his own advice in detail and with passion. 'Poppy . . .'

'Here,' Tim said as though tipping and held the money out. No difficulty this time. The note vanished agreeably as though it had never been offered.

Jimmy put his hand on Tim's shoulder. 'That's the boy then . . .'

Poppy, in the car, raised a hand; Jimmy raised a hand. To her. Perhaps they, at least, understood each other. Bertrand asked: 'Is that the "trainer"? '

'It used to be,' Poppy said. 'Now he trains cockroaches.'

Jakey saluted and moved back towards the car.

Maureen was looking at Tim. He looked down at a chip out of the step on which she was standing and gave the old stone scar a vague kick. As usual something was missing. Something so vast that it was no wonder he could never *catch* it so as to see what it was. So let it stay that way.

'Are you going then . . . ?' Maureen said.

He faced her for a moment.

'That seems to be the general idea . . .'

'Ta-ta then,' she said at last.

He scratched his head, closing his eyes and then swung away from her, back to the car. When it moved he didn't look back.

36

'Quite a priddy girl,' his father laughed.

'Straight to the boat?' Jakey said.

Tim said: 'Yes, please.'

Poppy said, 'You ought to have taken her with you.' She was cheering up with every yard that increased her distance from Light Street and from the further explosion from Bertrand which she had dreaded. 'Why not? Little playmate. Give her a bath. Polish her up a bit. Little carbolic soap and a coat of paint. She'd be just the thing for the journey. What . . .' She made herself laugh the more so as Bertrand encouraged her by smiling. 'Is he blushing?' she went on and leant forward and sideways to see his cheek.

Tim opened the big blade of his pocket-knife . . .

'God,' she cried, 'look at that, he is blushing—*he's in love!*'

A young person who seldom opens his mouth without giving the impression that he was reaching the end of some obscure tether might be regarded as the safest bet for permanent teasing. After all, soaks are supposed never to get drunk. Poppy therefore had no expectation of what now happened.

Tim whipped round and raised the knife over her head. At the same instant Jakey's free hand caught his wrist. Then there was his father's voice saying, 'Tim—sit down . . . drop that.'

He would, he really would have liked to.

And somehow they knew his wish.

Even Poppy. She stared at him with dark, piercing saucer eyes as though now she really would never forgive his ingratitude, his nutty behaviour . . . and the fright he had just given her.

She had loved him; *she* would never have sent him away. Oh, the ingratitude! No wonder she stared at him as she did. He deserved to be punished a bit.

A few moments passed. Suddenly she muttered, 'Proof!' Duff barked and she brought the dog up to her neck, hiding her face in him, inhaling his coat and murmuring, through tears: 'Thank heavens we've got one sane little guy.'

'Sit round, Tim,' Jakey said quietly.

Tim collapsed, faced forward, looking at funnels. They drove on. Bertrand muttered something to himself.

Suddenly Jakey began to speak as though remembering some long quotation with difficulty, 'I always get excited at the prospect of a sea-voyage . . . How about you, Tim? . . . I think it must be something very old in us, inherited from countless generations, from people for whom a voyage across the ocean really was a voyage . . .'

'God!' Poppy protested. 'What's this!'

But after a pause Jakey went on: 'Now I come to think of it you're rather like those people: for you the horizon really is a horizon, a mere line, always there, day after day. Suddenly it will thicken into roughness, little bumps and nobs. You'll see birds . . . That's the moment I love. And then there it is—an unknown country. Everything's new, fresh. You find a life of which you had no conception among people you've never met . . . You'll be a stranger but not for very long.'

Poppy suddenly laughed as though remembering a dream. 'He nearly knifed me. He *did*!'

Jakey heard but went on:

'You're lucky in one way. You're an Ambassador . . .

No, I mean that, Tim . . . You can help bring them in on our side. Women and children were often used as ambassadors by beleaguered cities. A bit soppy—but it worked.'

Tim thought: *Supposing I had!*

'They're nuts on bombs,' Jakey went on. 'Just tell them you were bombed and they'll run you for President. And you'll make friends for life . . .'

Tim was glad of that quiet, insistent voice. In time he looked about him and became aware of the still-open knife in his hand and put it away as inconspicuously as possible: then aware of the heavy coat round his shoulders and vaguely of the effect it had had on everyone; how it had finally even brought his father here to the dockside to see him off.

He frowned, bewildered, even by his own feelings which were quite contradictory, on the one hand exulting in the significant weight of this coat and on the other again wishing he had lost it, yes. Just to teach them! Of course he had no idea what it was he wanted to teach them, but the idea of them being utterly deprived *now* of *what they wanted most* gave him, now that Jakey's voice had stopped, the nearest feeling he could get to satisfaction.

They stopped and a sentry came towards them. Bertrand began wheeling down the window, leaning forward impatiently, saying, 'Where's Naughton? I told him to meet us here.'

The man in question managed to reach the door handle at that moment, in time.

37

Not far from Light Street there is, or used to be, a long shopping centre and in it an Italian tailors called Nello which sold off-the-peg clothes. Here Maureen entered that same afternoon and asked to see the men's sports jackets. The two attendants stared at her as though she had lost her way and the oldest coped with her as though conferring a favour. But she jerked her hair back, chewed her gum, and pushed out a five-pound note.

When they showed her the row of utility coats she advanced straight to one and touched it as though there must be some mistake. She had never expected to find the same one. Her fingers pinched the edge a bit, as they had pinched the edge of the other before giving it in at the hotel. The difference was the same as between a carpet and cloth. Yes, she said, she'd have that one. She got five shillings change and walked out into darkening streets, with the parcel under her arm.

A ship mourned somewhere behind the buildings, behind the mist, and she stopped. She could hear the violent wash of tugs and sensed rather than heard the throb of engines, like a pulse inside herself.

At that moment Tim was leaning over a ship's rail. Beside him stood a stiff little girl in pigtails and a smiling woman with a grey bun and a big handbag full of documents and First Aid. The gangways were being wound in. Far down, diminished, among the coils of rope stood a group of three people none of them standing very close to each other, Jakey a bit in the background now suddenly saluting, Poppy to one side weeping with an abandon which Tim found somehow irrelevant and irritating. Had he not seen her break down like this before—outside Caxton Hall on the occasion of her marriage to his father? He had, and could make no connection between that event and this. But then what connection was there between anything? His father also had taken out a handkerchief. Tim had a fleeting, lunatic impulse to take off his coat and drop it into the oily gap of water which was now increasing foot by foot, between the pier and the ship's side.

Instead he took out his coloured souvenir of the Edgware Road, the smutty coloured ball which the crane had managed, and threw it into the increasing gap. A gull shied at it and another followed it to check on its edibility: the wind took it to water well astern, not far from where his relations were standing. They all saw it. After a moment's hesitation he saw Poppy, still holding a flimsy handkerchief near her nose, point at the ball and make some suggestion to Jakey. He affected not to hear, still raising his arm in salute; but Poppy had made herself laugh, through her tears, encouraging her to wave again and hold up Duff, suddenly, like a peace-offering after what had happened in the car . . . 'the tantrum with the knife' she reminded him, four years later.

He did not need reminding. But by then he had listed the episode along with fossils—precisely—as proof, if proof were necessary, that all emotion is 'somewhat akin to madness and best given as wide a berth as possible.' Certainly for him the berth widened over the years. He became a well-known collector, an 'exquisite,' and was a familiar figure at Sothebys; he never married. He took a degree in archæology and wrote a thesis on 'racial senescence.' Later he set about killing himself, deliberately it seemed with drink, rich, isolated, cranky, sought after by people of both sexes. He took melancholy pleasure in deriding their love for him, or at the suggestion that from his life something was missing.

And of course he became the Earl of Bewick. His father had been right.

Peter was killed, late in 1941 in a raid on Peenemunde. The ticker-tape welcome which Tim had prophesied for him was enjoyed by others—and witnessed by Tim himself, in Wall Street, standing beside the man who had 'fielded' the coat, four years earlier, a man incidentally who had provided Tim in holiday time with plenty of what his father had foretold, 'priddy girls and popcorn.'

After research from London Jakey sent Father Doyle a hundred pounds for the Lennox family. He himself was killed at Alamein having cheated the army doctors about his heart. He left his fortune to Poppy and owing to his death at the hands of the enemy it was lightly taxed.

Poppy then left Bertrand and married a young Italian, also called Bert, in spite of being Italian.

Poppy kept a vignetted picture of Jakey beside one of Duff for several years on her Adam mantelpiece in Hampshire. Then Duff had the place to himself. She dislikes the macabre and lives in the present. Jimmy did not live to see Armistice day but Maureen married a G.I. and has two children in California. One of them by some curious alchemy of the mind, she called Tim.